Beyond Any

By

Tom Phelan

"The only truth is love beyond reason"
Alfred de Mussett

For Kathy - Mo Chuisle

County Kilburn...

It was dark and cold in the old warehouse where he was lying on the floor.

"Wake up, wake up! They're coming!" the voice whispered loudly into Joe's ear. It was a woman's voice with a hint of an accent. He was dazed but the voice seemed familiar to him as he came round.

He was lying face down on a damp wooden floor; the room smelled old and musty, and he heard something, a rat or a mouse, scurry across the floor nearby.

"Hurry, you must go now. Wake up before they find you!" The woman's voice, though still a whisper, was getting louder and louder.

He blinked a couple of times then opened his eyes slowly.

"Where the fuck am I?" he said, watching his breath as it plumed out onto the cold night air. He felt bad that he had sworn at this woman.

As he pulled his shoulder up from the cold wooden floor, he felt a sharp excruciating pain coming from his right hand. He lifted it up to his face and looked at the mass of congealed blood that surrounded a black gaping wound, then he started to remember what had happened earlier, vivid flashbacks of extreme violence, shock and pain.

"Quickly! You must go, they are coming now!" the whisper in his ear continued. He could feel her cold breath on the side of his cheek as she urged him to leave. He sat up, shook his head and looked up at the dark, starry sky through the large skylight, then slowly he turned his head towards the lady that had awakened him.

"Where am I?" he asked her, shaking his head. There was no one there. Then he heard the sirens...

1

Eleven months later...

Sitting on a wooden bench in the empty changing room and breathing deeply with a damp towel over his head, Joe Fitzpatrick waited for Frank to come in and tell him the truth, the inevitable truth, that they both knew but one of them didn't want to hear.

Joe had known Francis Dunne, better known as Frank or Frankie, since he was a kid, from the first day he and his best mate Danny Grealish had wandered into Frank's boxing club, St Anthony's, in Kilburn.

Danny and boxing never really got on. Frankie used to say, "He tries hard the kid, but he can't fight sleep." Frequently getting dropped or hurt in the ring and to much piss taking from the other lads, Danny eventually decided to swap boxing for Pilates. He was tired of getting beaten up and valued his looks too much. He loved boxing but boxing never really liked Danny.

Joe on the other hand was a natural. From a London-Irish family, Joe's dad Jimmy, and his dad's brother Uncle Micky, had both boxed. Micky was the more successful of the two, progressing through the amateur ranks to represent London, then followed a brief career in the paid version of the sport fighting on good undercards, but it ended abruptly for him when he stepped in as a late replacement to fight an unknown, classy, heavyweight Yank on an undercard at The York Hall in Bethnal Green. Uncle Mick was naturally a light heavyweight, and because he was making the jump up to heavyweight there would be no struggle to make weight. He could be as heavy as he wanted to be. So, with making the weight not an issue, Micky ignored two of the most basic rules in boxing:

1. Before a fight you have to train regularly, even if you don't have to make weight.

2. If you decide to ignore rule 1, you can't just go on the piss instead.

The one-sided fight ended brutally in the fifth round, a detached retina and broken eye socket ensuring that Mick would never fight again. Pilates wasn't an option for Uncle Micky.

So Mick had come through the usual apprenticeship that qualified you to bounce on the doors of a variety of Cricklewood and Kilburn establishments, greeting people, happy that they wanted to share their memories, a lot of them made up, of his fights. They talked of his great tear ups, some of them in places he had never been to in his life, but Mick just nodded, happy that they'd buy him a drink and wanted his company. But as time went on nobody remembered his fights anymore and he ended up losing his final one with the bottle just as his younger brother Jimmy had a few years earlier.

The classy heavyweight Yank that ended Uncle Micky's career went on to fight for a world title.

The paid game...

Joe took to boxing from the moment he stepped into St Anthony's, and it showed. A southpaw with a heavy left hand, he soon started knocking over older guys in the gym and, as he rose through the amateur ranks, he got paid work by going to other camps sparring contenders that needed southpaws to prepare them for "cack handed" fighters.

At twenty-two Joe won the ABA's at middleweight, but when the time came to box for a chance to go to the Olympics he opted to go professional. His mum was struggling on her own and an Olympic medal, whatever the colour, wouldn't suffice for months of unpaid rent.

3

The Troubles...

Concetta Frances Clarke, or Connie as everyone called her, had arrived in London from Dublin during the turbulent seventies, following her fiancé Jimmy Fitzpatrick across the sea. England at that time was a country in the middle of political unrest and young Connie found herself in the heart of a capital city full of power cuts, strikes and picket lines.

It was also during "The Troubles" and the IRA bombings of London were at their height, causing a deep national hostility towards Irish people and their communities. Connie witnessed this anti-Irish sentiment first-hand when, one cold January day, she was standing in the queue at a greengrocer holding a bowl of potatoes waiting for them to be weighed. It was the day after bombs had been detonated in Oxford Street setting Selfridges ablaze. On hearing Connie's accent the greengrocer turned to her and said loudly, "I see your lot have been at it again, Paddy."

Connie looked at the man and felt every pair of eyes in the room on her as she calmly replied, "Listen, every country has a terrorist organisation and yours is the National Front!" Then she launched the King Edwards across the floor and stormed out.

Jimmy Fitzpatrick had arrived in London a couple of years earlier, and after spending time hopping from one part of London to another he finally settled in Kilburn, or County Kilburn as the Irish population of the area had named it.

It was traditional among these Irish refugees for the man of the relationship to go ahead and find work in England,

4

then send for their partner to "come across the water" to join them.

Jimmy was a good electrician and he found it fairly easy to job hop across various building sites in order to check locations out to find where he wanted to put down his roots, and Kilburn with its large Irish community worked for him, plus his older brother Micky had already settled in neighbouring Cricklewood.

Jimmy and Connie were married in 1977 on the day that Red Rum won his third Grand National, and the next year their only child Joseph was born. The couple had an increasingly turbulent marriage that got tougher when Jimmy's drinking habit grew out of control in his late thirties, to the point where he was unable to hold a job down. As Jimmy's health declined so the debts grew and between Connie and Joe they tried to cover them, but Jimmy's drink problem extended to years of unpaid bills that Connie thought had been paid, with the money spent on whiskey instead.

When Jimmy eventually died of cirrhosis his legacy was to leave his wife close to ruin. Connie passed away the following year following a stroke. The worry had killed her.

The chase...

Unlike a lot of amateurs Joe took to the pro game instantly. Swapping point scoring for brutal knockouts, he won the southern area title in his sixth fight and soon it was hard to get a fight for the hard-hitting southpaw from North West London. He had managers and promoters banging his door down so it should have been easy for Joe to go through the ranks, but it wasn't.

Joe's promoter was Frank's brother, Liam Dunne, known to everyone as Billy. Joe had known Billy almost as long as he'd known Frank. They had looked after a very vulnerable teenage lad when his dad Jimmy died, and throughout his dad's long booze related illness kept Joe from going off the rails. They were good, honest men.

The problem is at the top end of boxing there is no room for good, honest men.

Joe wanted to fight the skilful, unbeaten Scot George Wallace for Wallace's British super middleweight title. Joe knew it was a tough fight but he saw cracks in Wallace's game. He dropped his right hand when he threw a left hook for a start, perfect for a southpaw with a heavy left hand. Joe needed the Wallace fight to move on to where the money was, European, and then, potentially, world level.

While Joe's mates were pissing away their twenties Joe trained like a demon taking and winning whatever fight he was offered, glad of the distraction as without boxing he was terrified of what his life would turn into. He needed something to focus on. He had enough mates with drink and drug problems, some whiling away their broken lives in the nick and a few that succumbed to knife and gun crimes and were no longer around.

When Joe wasn't training he would be found with his head in a book as his old man had instilled a love of literature into him and he grew up on Jimmy Fitzpatrick's taste for Irish literature. The works of Brendan Behan, Sean O'Casey, James Joyce and Flann O'Brien were devoured. He read and reread *Borstal Boy*, taking in Behan's autobiographical experience as a young IRA recruit captured in possession of explosives in a Liverpool of different times, as well as the posthumously published sequel *Confessions of an Irish Rebel*. He later marvelled at the writing of Charles Dickens. Oliver Twist's London was fascinating to him, as was Thomas Hardy's Wessex with its tragic tale of *Tess of the D'Urbevilles*.

Joes passion for boxing and books kept him on the straight and narrow.

Every day though Joe would be on Frank and Billy's case. "I'm thirty-two now and I'm not getting any younger. Get me the Wallace fight, you know I can beat him," or "When are you gonna let me fight that Jock fuckpig? I could do with the dough."

Frank and Billy's stock reply was always, "Be patient, son, we're trying to sort it but it's taking time. Everything happens for a reason."

The harsh truth was that Joe was never going to get the Wallace fight. The Scotsman was promoted by the flamboyant Marc Harris, the biggest and most successful promoter in Britain and Europe.

Harris had wanted Joe to join his stable for a long time, regularly putting calls in to Joe and Frank and offering great money. Harris knew that on Joe's best day he would school Wallace, but he wasn't going to risk his fighter's British title going to another promoter. Harris also had the European super middleweight champ in his star-studded camp. So, unless Joe signed for Harris he wouldn't get a shot at any of the titles.

George Wallace was a gregarious character and he was living the life earning great money. With his rugged good looks he was made for the camera and he regularly appeared on TV as a pundit and even on reality shows.

Joe was tired of headlining small hall shows earning comparatively meagre sums for this extraordinarily dedicated, physically brutal job, but the harsh truth was that this was as far as Frank and Billy Dunne could take him. Then, one Friday afternoon, after a really gruelling sparring session, Joe turned on his little TV in his mum's old flat. He flicked through the channels as he opened up the debt letters then stopped. George Wallace's beaming mug was

7

on the celebrity version of the TV show *The Chase,* and as he watched Wallace being pursued for money by the chaser he finally snapped.

"Yeah, that's it, you chase the cunt!" He'd had enough. Joe grabbed his mobile and dialled the missed call number that he had received that morning.

Mayfair...

Marc Harris was having a late lunch at The Wolseley in Piccadilly with Matt Jacobs. Jacobs was just off the back of defending his WBC world heavyweight title at London's O2. Being a heavyweight and especially being "The Heavyweight Champion of the World", Jacobs was the star of Marc Harris's talented camp and made Harris a lot of money. "There's heavyweights and then there's the rest," Harris would frequently state when explaining his bias of affection towards Jacobs to the rest of his camp.

"Try it, champ, you'll love it," Harris said pointing to one of The Wolseley's signature dishes on the menu.

"But it's raw fucking meat," Jacobs replied. "I know I'm a fighter but I'm not a bleeding savage." Harris laughed.

"It's beef tartare, champ, it's only made with the best cuts of beef so you can eat it raw."

"Not for me, Marc, I'll stick with the well done version. I'll have the rib eye."

The pretty waitress came over in her traditional black and white uniform. "Are you ready to order, gentlemen?" she said with a heavy French accent. Just then Harris's mobile flashed up with the name of the London-Irish super middleweight that he'd been pursuing for years. As he pushed the button to answer it he could hear the pretty young waitress saying to Jacobs, "I saw your fight on Saturday, you were very good.

Knightsbridge...

Marc Harris's office was as ostentatious as the man himself and proof that money can't buy taste. The promoter beckoned towards his desk. "Sit down, Joe. Coffee?" Feeling a sense of betrayal to the Dunne brothers, Joe parked up on a padded, scarlet leather chair opposite Harris. A stuffed zebra's head disapprovingly looked down on him from the wall. Joe glared back at it.

Look, I need the dough, right? I feel bad enough being here as it is without you judging me, you fucking zebra cunt, Joe thought as he stared defiantly at the lifeless lump of taxidermy on the wall.

"Do you like it, Joe?" Harris said, noticing Joe looking at the zebra's head. "My grandfather shot it in Africa."

"Oh," Joe replied, "I just assumed he must've been running at some speed when he hit the other side of that wall." Harris smiled at Joe sympathetically.

Fuck me, thought Joe, *he ain't got the same sense of humour as Billy Dunne...*

Joe felt out of place in these surroundings like he didn't belong there, almost like he was a kid again, then, for whatever reason, he thought of his dad. *Would he have ever been somewhere like this? Only to rewire it...*

When he was growing up Joe used to spend most of his Saturdays and all his school holidays helping his dad out at work, and because of this Joe became a very good "sparks" in his own right and earned a few quid here and there by doing odd electrical jobs. It was a good trade to fall back on when the boxing finished.

Everywhere in Harris's office there were pictures of the promoter with famous people in swanky places. There were at least two prime ministers as well as an ageing Muhammad Ali, Barack Obama and Justin Bieber. It was a bit different to Billy Dunne's cramped office above a newsagent where Joe made his own tea, often having to go downstairs to buy the milk, with Billy's pictures of his grandkids sharing the walls with black and white photos of half famous greyhounds.

Joe and Mr Harris, "Please, call me Marc," talked for about an hour. "Glasgow's gonna be a hostile crowd, you're not worried about taking the fight up there?"

"No, Mr Harris." Joe had forgotten to call him Marc. "My punches will hurt just as much in Glasgow as they do in London." Harris smiled. He could see the pound signs in front of him.

Joe walked out of Harris's office with a three-fight deal in his pocket for fabulous money, including a ten grand cash advance (the safe was hidden, appropriately behind a picture of Harris shaking hands with the boxer Floyd 'Money' Mayweather) and an agreement to fight George Wallace at the SSE Arena in Glasgow for the British title in three months' time.

As he walked through the large, brass, glazed doors and outside into the fresh West London air, Joe should have been delighted. After all, this was what he'd been after since he first put the gloves on. He felt flat though. Yeah, he could clear his mum's debts and stay in the flat, but by signing that all binding contract using that gaudy gold pen with a ruby on the clip, he'd gone against everything he had held real and all the values he'd been brought up with. He was entering into a new world, a world of money, deceit and dishonesty, a world where he felt he didn't belong.

Kilburn...

St Anthony's Boxing Club was a good old-fashioned "spit and sawdust" gym, the whipping sound of the skipping ropes and the grunts and groans of heavy training punctuated every now and then by some punter coming in to sell snide Canada Goose coats or dodgy Ray Bans; there was a permanent background aroma of liniment and stale sweat.

Frank and Joe sat on the steps leading up to the entrance. Frank was rolling a fag when a builder's van tooted at them as it drove past. "Your dad was a good fighter, not as popular as your Uncle Micky, but he was a crafty fighter if you know what I mean? He had a great jab, even better than yours, and that set up his back hand. His footwork wasn't as good as yours though."

Frank said, "Whereas Micky used to just get in there and go straight through them, bang, bang, bang, no questions fuckin' asked." He threw a jab, right hand and left hook into the air in front of him as he said it, then chuckled to himself, which led to a short bout of chesty coughing. "I sparred them both a few times, and I probably learned more sparring your old man than your uncle." Joe watched Frank drawing on his roll-up, staring straight ahead and going through old ring wars in his head.

"Frank," Joe interrupted, "whereas you seem to have got the best of both of them, son..." " Frank, I need to talk to you". "You've got Micky's power and your dad's ring craft," "But there's something you don't know," Joe said, a little louder as another van went by and tooted at the pair.

"No, there isn't, son." Frankie turned and looked directly into Joe's eyes. "You've signed for Harris." Joe looked away. He was gutted that Frank had heard before he'd got the chance to tell him. "He rang me as soon as you left his office, fucker couldn't wait to tell me."

Edgware Road...

Danny Grealish's life had followed a different path to Joe's. He had helped out in his mum & dad's cafe "Rosa's" on Kilburn High Road since he was a young boy, and took over the running of it when he was eighteen when Davy, Danny's dad, who was a hard-working, slight man from Cork, died. His Italian mum Rosetta, known as Rosa, was a lovely, bubbly large lady who still helped Danny out now and then.

The Pilates that he gave up after getting punched in the face for evolved into yoga, and that holistic path led him to becoming a vegetarian and then a vegan. All Dan's mates took the piss out of him for his veganism. "Are you alright eating something that casts a shadow, Dan?" But he just laughed it off. He wasn't one of those preachy vegans that get on everyone's nerves.

Danny and Joe had known each other since they were at primary school together making their first Holy Communion on the same day and, although their lives took on very different paths, they still kept in touch all the time and every now and again they would catch up over a game of snooker at the local British Legion Club.

Danny had done really well at Rosa's, he'd converted it to an Italian deli and having outgrown the shop he ended up selling it to a local butchers. Staying in the food business, Dan acquired a large, struggling Turkish restaurant on Edgware Road down towards Marble Arch, refurbished it completely and reopened it as a vegan restaurant and yoga retreat called "Om Squad". Om Squad was smashing it, tapping into the high end, wellness warriors with money market.

"I heard you left Frank and Billy?" Danny said as he leant over the snooker table to play a red.

"I left Billy because I wasn't making any dough, Dan. Part of the deal was that I had to leave Frankie and hook up with one of Harris's trainers, as otherwise he said there would be a 'conflict of interest' or something like that."

"That must've been tough. You were with him since you were a kid. Hey, we joined on the same day, remember?"

"Yeah, it was tough. I love Frankie but you gotta earn money, right?" Joe was putting on a false show of bravado. It killed him to leave Frank and Danny knew it, so he backed off.

"Anyway, how's the avocado business going, Mahatma fuckin' Gandhi?" Joe asked laughing.

"It's going well, mate, really well, so well in fact that your mate rang me the other day showing an interest."

"Who's my mate?" asked Joe.

"Tommy Molloy." Joe stood up from his shot.

"Tommy Molloy? What did that melt want?"

"What do you fuckin' think?" Danny replied. "Asked me if I needed his firm to look after our security. He said the last thing we needed would be a fire, unless we were thinking of going into 'Hot Yoga', then he laughed at his own joke, the prick."

"What did you say?" Joe asked.

"I told him to fuck himself," Danny snapped back.

The Molloys...

The Molloy brothers were the crime family that "ran" North West London, and virtually any crime in the area could be traced back to them, their underlings or sycophants. The Molloy family controlled all the drug deals, loan sharking and protection rackets in the neighbourhood. They would lend money and demand interest at 3% weekly, so if you borrowed £5,000 you would pay them back £150 a week just in interest. Failure to pay back at least the interest every week would prompt a "visit" which normally ended up with the loanee having a leg or arm broken. Usually they would break the limb that you least needed to earn a living so you could still earn the money to pay them back the weekly interest.

Sean, Terry and Tommy Molloy were the three brothers that ran the gang. Tommy was the youngest, he was a couple of years above Joe and Danny at school, and they had no time for him then and less time for him since.

Tommy Molloy was a bully that liked to terrify local business owners with his demands for protection money. He was happiest in and around the Kilburn area where he was known and where he could use his Molloy "status" to feed his ego. He liked being a big fish in a smallish pond.

Had it not been for the fact that he was born into this vicious family, he would have gone the way that a lot of the other local lads who had left school with no qualifications had gone, lapsing into drink and drug problems. He would probably have ended up in prison or dead, but instead of that and because of his brothers he was "a face".

Terry Molloy was the quietest of the three siblings. He was happiest in the background and, unlike the other two, didn't really frequent any of their "operations" unless he was needed to. The quietest brother though was also the most vicious. His "party trick" was to bite the nose off anyone who crossed him, and his arrival on any potential crime scene always put the fear of God into those that were about to be meted out with some of the Molloys' rough justice.

Sean Molloy was the main man, the eldest and most feared of the brothers. He had wanted Joe to "muscle" for him for a long time, collecting so-called debts, debts meaning money owed by innocent business owners who were too scared not to pay for the reassurance of knowing that their business, or house, wouldn't be burned down or destroyed. Sean had plans to expand into other locations as he thought they had outgrown North West London and was keen to move their business into the West End. He liked the glamour of places like Soho and Piccadilly and was becoming a bit of a "player" on the celebrity circuit; actors, singers, politicians and even those high up in Scotland Yard and MI5 were keen to rub shoulders with the charming, glamorous gangster.

Sean Molloy knew Frankie Dunne. He had trained at St Anthony's years earlier, but after three years he suddenly stopped going. He was always asking Frank to get Joe involved with his mob in their gutter business. Joe could never work for the Molloys, the local working-class people had their opinion of the Molloy family and what they did to hard-working families in the area.

"You told him to fuck himself? Seriously?" Joe asked Danny.

"Yeah, I told him to fuck himself."

"What did he say?" Joe was worried for his oldest mate.

"He just said, 'Okay, Hot Yoga it is then,' and hung up."

Euston...

Joe was sent to train with one of Harris's trainers, Dave Nelson, at his gym "Toe 2 Toe" in Drummond Street behind Euston Station.

To say it was different to St Anthony's Gym in Kilburn was the biggest understatement since Noah looked out of the Ark and said, "It's raining."

As they walked through the gymnasium's Juice Bar and into the changing rooms, Nelson said, "This is your locker

15

key, Joe," handing Joe what looked like a credit card. "This card opens and locks it."

Joe took the card and looked at the locker. "In all the years I've boxed I never had my own locker, let alone one that opens with a bleeding Barclaycard."

The gym was all glass and chrome with futuristic-looking training kit. Joe had no idea what some of the kit was for, they looked like something out of a torture chamber. There were showers with hot water, celebrities doing pads, there were even women training there, and at Toe 2 Toe the Canada Goose coats and Ray Bans were real.

Dave Nelson was a very good trainer, he had been a good amateur boxer himself and had a successful pro career as Davy "Horatio" Nelson, cleaning up domestically and eventually fighting for a world title. As a trainer he had handled some very good fighters and got a few of them to world level, so he was a perfect fit for Joe. He was a nice fella as well, there was nothing not to like. Dave Nelson and Joe hit it off straight away, it would never be the same as with Frankie Dunne, but they worked well together and Joe enjoyed the challenge of learning the different training techniques after all the years he had been training at St Anthony's.

As well as Dave, Joe was sorted out with a conditioning coach, a nutritionist and the best sparring partners, and there were press conferences coming up to promote the fight, open sparring sessions and interviews with the media. It was a different world and Joe lapped it up.

Hyde Park...

Training at Toe 2 Toe was going really well. Dave Nelson, along with his conditioning coach and nutritionist, had Joe feeling in the best shape of his life. He was at a press conference in The Four Seasons Hotel, Hyde Park, to announce the fight with George Wallace.

"Just be yourself," Dave Nelson advised Joe as they walked through the doors to be greeted by the press, loads of them.

Fuck me, Joe thought when he saw how much interest this fight had generated. They headed towards a long table with jugs of water laid out on it and little name cards in front of each seat. Joe could see Wallace and his trainer sat at the far end with Marc Harris sat in the centre and two empty seats to Harris's left. Behind the table there was a huge banner hanging on the wall proclaiming *"The Battle of Britain"* with a picture of George Wallace with blue and white face paint on to make him look like his namesake William Wallace. Joe was done up as a pilot from the Second World War with a spitfire behind him and a Labrador at his feet.

Joe and Dave sat down, Joe next to Harris with Dave Nelson beside him. Wallace was on the other side of the promoter. Joe couldn't wait for the face-off at the end, it was the first time he had seen Wallace in the flesh and he wanted to size him up, and although he was sitting down he didn't look as big as he thought he would.

Marc Harris ran through the preliminaries. He was in his element Joe thought, probably overdid it a bit with the hair dye though, "as full of himself as a Russian doll," as Billy Dunne once described him. Joe smiled at the memory as Harris was thanking a long list of people and sponsors. Then it was time for questions from the press.

"How do you see the fight going, George? Do you think you can stop him?" Wallace looked up.

17

"Fitzpatrick's a decent, domestic fighter, but he's thirty-two years old and this game's all about levels. He's been fighting blokes that I wouldn't give sparring to. He isn't at my level, so no, it won't go the distance."

"What about you, Joe, same question to you?" Joe's mouth was dry as he looked over at Wallace.

"On his best day and my best day I stop him." Joe took a sip of water. "And on his best day and my worst day I win unanimously on points." There was laughter from some of the press and this got up Wallace's nose.

"You've never done what I've done."

"No, you're right, George," said Joe cutting him off. "I've never dressed up as Braveheart for an Iron fuckin' Brew advert." Joe kept a straight face while the press laughed. He caught sight of Danny at the back of the room and winked at him. Dan was laughing and gave him a nod of approval. When they went for the face-off Joe noticed he was about an inch taller than Wallace despite all the records making them the same height. They stared into each other's eyes with the tips of their noses touching.

"Gonna batter you, ya anglish cant!" Wallace snarled.

"Have a day off, you Scottish melt!" Joe replied. Wallace pushed Joe back and before Joe could get after him the security men jumped in between them.

That's it, job done. The fighters had done their bit hyping the fight, now they could go back to training and let the media run with it until the next presser in a week's time in Glasgow.

Edgware Road...

Joe sat at a table looking around. Om Squad was very stylish and there was a large sign above him proclaiming *"Let food be your medicine"*. The walls had been cleverly painted to look as if they were distressed and from an old school gymnasium, and areas were made to look like the paint was cracking and peeling with the previous colour showing through and fading lines running along the walls. It was busy with a clientele that looked as though they would much rather be barefooted.

"Place looks good, Dan, it's a bit like the old gym at school," Joe said. "I was gonna get the apparatus out," they laughed.

"Yeah, it cost a lot of money to make it look this shit, Joe."

"Fuck me, the old man would've been proud of you, Danny boy."

The "old man", Davy Grealish, was the victim of an attempted robbery at Rosa's when Danny was eighteen. He had been working late on a Thursday night when some blokes turned up to rob the cafe. Davy wasn't a big man but he refused to give over the week's takings and was knifed to death in the ensuing fight. They never caught the assailants and for a long time it was linked by the locals to the Molloy family.

Joe had come over to meet Danny who had phoned to say he had a threatening letter put through the letterbox. Joe sipped on a blueberry maple shake that looked like something to do with mealworms on a bushtucker trial but tasted okay.

"I saw Frankie Dunne the other day outside the bookies next to Grace O'Malley's," Dan said.

"How was he?"

"He was fine considering he'd just done his bollocks on a dog that Billy got a tip for," Joe laughed.

"Same old, same old. Did he mention me at all?"

"Yeah, I told him I'd heard. He just shrugged and said, 'I'm glad for the kid, he'll go well, deserves it, he was too good for me to keep hold of.' He was fine."

"So this was put through the letterbox." Danny handed Joe an A4 piece of paper folded over. He opened it up to reveal a flyer with the heading "HOT YOGA CLASSES" with a match sellotaped to it.

"This was posted to here?"

"No, to my house. It was put through the letterbox by hand," Dan replied.

"What did Karen say?" Joe asked.

"She never saw it. She was out and I haven't told her. It would worry her too much."

Karen Moore was Danny's girlfriend. They lived together having met when they were at school. Joe took her twin sister Kim out for a couple of years from when he was nineteen. He really liked her and she was one of the few girls that could make him laugh, taking the piss out of him all the time which other girls were too wary to do because of his profession. It didn't work out though as the hours Joe had to spend in the gym and strict dietary requirements meant they had no real social life, and Kim was too young to sacrifice a social life in her late teens and early twenties for the potential contender. Joe's "black Irish" looks, black hair with dark eyes and boxer's physique made him a target for the fairer sex, but with his devotion to living the boxer's life apart from Kim his love life consisted only of two or three-week affairs and one-night stands.

When Karen and Kim's parents split up Karen moved in with Danny and Kim moved to Spain with her mum, Bridget, to Mijas on the Costa del Sol, the theory being that the warm weather would help Kim's mum with her crippling rheumatoid arthritis. Karen's decision to stand by her philandering dad and Kim's decision to emigrate caused a massive rift between the sisters and they hadn't spoken since, each of them relying on their mum for updates on the other. These updates had got fewer and fewer as the girls' mum had also been diagnosed with dementia.

Joe always felt that Kim could've been the one for him and was sad when she moved away. He always asked after her whenever he saw Karen and the last he heard she'd got knocked up, ironically by a mixed race, ex-pat boxer who had no intention of hanging around to see the fruits of his labour.

Joe's pugilistic lifestyle always got in the way of his love life. Long hours at the gym where he felt most at home, six or seven days a week, was not conducive to any kind of long-term relationship. So Danny had Karen and Joe had boxing.

"So what are you gonna do, Dan?"

"I'm not giving them a penny. I've worked fuckin' hard to get all this." He looked proudly around the restaurant as a couple of women with yoga mats under their arms walked past. "Why would I give it to them thieving cunts?"

"But it's not gonna go away, Dan." Joe looked hard at his oldest friend.

"You know how it works, Joe. I give them five hundred quid a week, then six months down the line they up it to a grand and so it goes on and on." Dan glared at Joe. "And it ain't just that, you know it ain't." Joe's thoughts went to Davy Grealish.

How the fuck could Danny give them a penny? They murdered his old man. "You can't go to the old bill, Dan"

"I know that. The Molloys are the old bill round here. I'm not stupid, Joe, if I did that I may as well set light to the fucking place myself!"

"Giuseppe!" Joe smiled as he turned around to see Danny's mum wearing an apron and walking towards him from the kitchen, her arms outstretched and a big smile on her face. Joe was shocked when he saw Rosa. He hadn't

21

seen her for a while and he remembered a big, bubbly, typical Italian mama, the Rosa walking towards Joe was probably a third of the size of the woman he remembered so fondly who used to force feed him at every opportunity.

"Hello, Rosa, how are you?" She gave Joe a big hug.

"Not so bad. How's my little Giuseppe?" she said, looking up at him. "You're so skinny, let me get you something to eat, not that anything from this kitchen would fatten you up," she said looking accusingly at Danny. Then she whispered loudly into Joe's ear, "I have some of my meatballs in the kitchen, I bring them in every day but nobody eats them. Let me go and heat them up for you.

"You can't bring them out into the restaurant, Momma," Danny laughed, pointing around the room. "Half of this lot would faint."

"Faint? They already look ill. Look at them, miserable all of them, they could do with some healthy, happy food, not animal's food. They love the animals so much, so why do they eat their food? Some nice Italian meatballs with parmesan?" Danny looked at Joe, smiled and raised his eyes.

"What chance have I got, Joe?" Joe laughed.

"That's right, Mrs G, they're miserable-looking. Make them smile and get some healthy food into them. Hide some mozzarella under the nut cutlets."

"You see?" Rosa said, pointing at Danny accusingly. "Even Giuseppe agrees with me." Danny kicked Joe under the table just as Joe's phone rang.

"Shi…" Joe stopped himself before he completed a swear word in front of Rosa. "Gotta go, got a sparring session." He kissed Rosa. "Danny, I'll give you a call," grabbed his kitbag and ran out of Om Squad. Joe knew what he had to do.

Kilburn...

Walking back into St Anthony's was hard for Joe. He always knew going back to the place he had spent most of his youth was going to be tough. Frankie was at the far end of the gym mopping the floor. He looked up when he heard Joe coming through the door, then looked down and carried on mopping. "Hello, Frank."

"What do you fuckin' want?"

Joe wasn't surprised by Frank's barked reply. This was a man who had virtually raised him as a son and looked after him way more than a trainer should have to look after a fighter.

"I'm sorry, Frank, I umm..." Joe stuttered.

Frank interrupted him. "I'm fucking about, Joe. Can't say I blame you, it's not like I could've got you the Wallace fight. It's a shame I had to hear it from Harris though, you should've told me before you went. I'd have understood..." Frank focused on Joe, then laughingly added, "...eventually."

Joe and Frank talked for a while, Frank talking him through a few of the up and coming fighters he had in the gym. Joe talked about things at Toe 2 Toe and the different way they did things. "It's mad, Frank. I'm on the treadmill the other day watching *X Factor* on the big screen and the bird that won it last year is on the rowing machine next to me. Fucking mental."

"Yeah, the only celebrities we get in here," Frank replied, "are the ones on Jeremy Kyle." They laughed then Joe got to the purpose of why he was there. "If you're sure you wanna do this I'll set it up," Frank said, as he looked out of the barred window of his tiny office at the back of the gym. "But I'm not happy about it. Be careful, these people, they're not like us, they're scumbags."

The meet up...

"D'you know what, son? When I was at school I got bullied, right, bullied something terrible. Yeah, that's right, me, Sean Molloy, bullied at school. Can you believe it?" Joe sat across a large hardwood desk looking at North West London's most notorious bully.

Sean Molloy cut an imposing figure, a large handsome man with receding, reddish hair that was greying at the temples. He was always tanned and immaculately dressed and groomed, his teeth were white enough to give Marc Harris's pristine railings a run for their money, and as he spoke Joe was drawn towards his gesticulating hands that, though well manicured, were covered in old scarring.

"I didn't have much but what I had they took, took the food out of my mouth sometimes, any money I had, the fuckin' lot." Joe just stared back across the wooden table. "But d'you know what I did? I fought back."

Joe had seen the eldest Molloy brother a few times, usually surrounded by either or both of his siblings, a variety of henchmen and numerous sycophants, as he swaggered through clubs and bars, usually in his camel hair coat flexing his muscles. But this time it was different. It was just him and Joe face to face in Sean's "office" above The Lord Nelson pub on Kilburn High Road.

"There was no use talking to the teachers, they'd just give you a clip round the ear and tell you to grow up and get on with it, so d'you know what I did?" He stared into Joe's eyes. "I grew up and got fuckin' on with it. Best advice you could get, teachers were proper then, not like they are now, they're not even allowed to tell a kid off anymore let alone give them a clip round the ear. Same with the old bill, world's gone fuckin' stupid." He stared at Joe expecting a reaction. Normally he'd get an agreeable response from one or more of his hangers-on, but Joe just

24

stared back impassively. "That's what you have to do," said the bully, "don't cry like a baby, get fuckin' on with it! Now, what do you fuckin' want? Suppose you've changed your mind about doing some muscle for me? Knew you'd come to your senses. I could do with someone like you. People know who you are around here, should shit them up a bit when they see you, sends out the right message. Pay what you owe or you get it." Sean half lifted off his seat and extended his arm towards Joe, then stroked him affectionately on the cheek. "Welcome on board, handsome." Joe flinched at the amorous gesture. *What was that about?*

"Danny Grealish," said Joe, pulling his head back, still seated, while Sean, taken aback and now looking uncomfortable, retracted his hand quickly and sat back down.

"Davy Grealish's boy?" the bully asked. "Got some poncy gaff down the Edgware Road. What about him?" Molloy looked confused.

"Your Tommy's put the hammer on him for protection."

"Well what d'you want me to do about it?" Sean shouted, embarrassed that he'd misread the situation and suddenly getting very animated. "He needs to just fuckin' pay it!"

"That's what I've come to see you about, Mr Molloy." Joe pulled out a stuffed white envelope and offered it towards him. Molloy looked at it.

"The fuck's that?"

"There's three grand there, take it and leave Danny alone. He's worked hard to get that place, with what happened to his old man and all." Molloy looked down derisively at the bulging envelope sat on the desk.

Joe watched as Molloy took a deep intake of breath. He had heard about his explosive temper and now, by embarrassing Molloy, it looked like he was about to witness it first-hand. Sean's whole frame seemed to expand.

25

"Is this a fuckin' wind up? Have you come here to insult me, is that it? You're brave, son, I'll give you that, brave but fucking stupid. If Tommy wants to legitimately offer his security services – which is his living by the way – to any companies around here, then that's called enterprise in my book. And fair play to him, your mate gives him dough and Tommy's security company look after the kid's assets for him." There was spittle shooting from his angry mouth. "Supply and fucking demand they call it!"

Joe swallowed. This hadn't gone the way he hoped it would and he knew this was only going to get worse the more he tried to talk to the bully. Sean Molloy's temper was notorious and Joe could see it building up. It was a mistake coming here to try and reason with the unreasonable.

"If you've got a problem with Tommy sort it out with him, or are you fucking scared of him, you toerag? Well, are you fucking scared of him, you muggy cunt?" Sean was goading Joe. *It's like he wants me to have a straightener with Tommy,* thought Joe. "Instead of that you turn up here to insult me? Now, how do you think it's gonna look you topping up here to tell me that your mate ain't gonna be paying what he owes? How do you think it's gonna look when you walk out of here past my blokes? I'll tell you how, like I've gone soft, you fuckin' maggot!"

This wasn't a situation Joe was comfortable with. He felt like a kid again being told off for doing something wrong. All he was doing was trying to look after his mate. He needed to get out of there and fast.

The Lord Nelson was a lively gastropub in the evenings, but during the day it was shut and used as a hangout for the Molloy gang, where their business was discussed and planned.

When Joe had arrived there for the meet-up that Frankie Dunne had arranged with Molloy, he had to walk through half a dozen of Molloy's heavies towards the narrow staircase in the far right corner of the bar that led to the office. They sniggered and looked trigger happy as he cut through them. Joe didn't relish the thought of pushing through them again on the way out.

As Joe made a move to get up and leave, Molloy suddenly pulled a short cosh from under the desk and swung at Joe who ducked to his right, the cosh brushing his left ear. Joe came up instinctively unloading a right hook to Molloy's temple, followed by a straight left through his face breaking his nose in the process and sending him careering backwards into a large bookcase of unread books.

Sean Molloy collapsed in a heap on the floor and groaned as a hardback copy of Dostoevsky's *Crime & Punishment* bounced off his forehead, the irony being lost in the moment.

Fuck! thought Joe. *The fuck did I do that for? I'm fucked.* He heard jolted, heavy movement downstairs which suggested people running towards the stairs. He looked around. There was a slightly opened sash window, and without thinking he pulled it fully open and jumped through it, dropping ten feet down onto the beer garden at the rear of The Lord Nelson. As he landed his ankle turned and he rolled over landing on his shoulder, his phone flying out of his jacket pocket and smashing on the cobbles. He picked himself up leaving the shattered phone and ran, limping, through the back exit from the pub garden, pushing over an A-board in front of the gate that proudly proclaimed in chalk text *"New Vegan Menu Coming Soon!"* He hurriedly limped round a corner and on to the busy Kilburn High Road, merging in with the shoppers, workers and vagrants. The bulging white envelope containing the remainder of his training expenses from Marc Harris was still sat on Molloy's desk.

Edgware Road...

"So where is he then?" Danny Grealish looked up. Dan was writing out the day's menu for Om Squad on a chalk board when Sean Molloy walked in, his signature long camel coat draped around his shoulders like a cape, a plaster across the bridge of his nose and two puffed up black eyes spoiling his otherwise immaculate appearance.

"I dunno, Sean, no fuckin' idea. I've tried calling him but his phone's dead. He's vanished."

"He doesn't know about this place, does he?"

"No, Sean, he ain't got a clue."

Sean looked down at Dan. "He's a dead man, Danny, Joe Fitzpatrick is a dead man." Danny looked back at Molloy and nodded. *How the fuck has it come to this?* "If anyone's gonna find him it's you, you know him better than anyone. Find out where he is and let me know! Understand? Or all this goes," Sean said, arms open wide and looking around Om Squad. "And it all comes out."

The men walked outside, shook hands after exchanging a few more words and embraced. Then Molloy got into the large, blue Bentley that was sat there blocking three other cars in. Danny looked furtively left and right before going back into Om Squad.

Had Danny Grealish looked straight ahead across the road and through the Starbucks window opposite, he'd have seen his oldest friend nursing a coffee, watching the two men on the other side of the road in discussion, shaking hands and embracing like they were the fucking Sopranos.

Cala de Mijas...

"When we find you, which we definitely will, you will be in so much trouble! We've already got two of your friends, and unless you come and see us they will be in big, big trouble too."

Elijah Moore sat there transfixed. He was now three years old and his dark eyes burned into the watercolour drawings on the book that Joe was reading to him. "'Okay, I'll come and see you,' said Billy Bunny, 'and I'm ever so sorry for eating your carrots.'" Joe looked across at Elijah. "'Okay, we'll let your friends go, but never do it again,' said Farmer Thomas."

Joe closed the hardback cover of *The Bunny Who Was Always in Trouble* and looked at Elijah. He was a good-looking little kid with a dark complexion, black wavy hair and deep brown eyes. "I'll read you the next bit tomorrow, little fella, now your mum wants to put you to bed." Kim came over and picked Elijah up, winked at Joe and carried the little bundle off to his small bedroom across the hall. It was almost two months since Joe had turned up at Kim Moore's apartment in Mijas, Spain.

When he saw Danny with Sean Molloy it broke Joe. He felt utterly betrayed by his oldest, closest friend. Why the fuck would Danny have anything to do with the Molloys? The Molloys who killed his old man, the Molloys who threatened to burn down his restaurant. Nothing made sense to Joe. He was only trying to help Dan and now he was a wanted man back in London, and even here on the Costa del Crime he may not be too safe.

When Joe landed on the cobbles in the yard of The Lord Nelson pub in Kilburn he damaged the lateral ligaments in his ankle. A Spanish doctor said he would not be able to train for two or three weeks. He rang Dave Nelson from a burner phone and told him the news. Nelson rang Marc Harris who was fuming.

29

"How am I gonna find someone at this late notice? Tell him I want my fucking dough back!" And the "Battle of Britain" between Joe and George Wallace was cancelled due to an "injury to Fitzpatrick while sparring". Wallace took on a late substitute, an older Italian journeyman, and walked through him in two rounds to the sound of booing from the Glasgow crowd. Marc Harris wasn't happy.

Now, for the first time since he was a young kid, boxing was not Joe's obsession anymore. He wanted to know what was going on with Danny, he wanted revenge for his robbed opportunity of fighting for the British title, for his three grand, but, much more than anything else, he wanted the Molloys, and he wanted Sean in particular. Boxing could wait, he was going to cut the head off the fucking snake.

Fourteen years earlier...

For all his calming holistic lifestyle, his veganism, Pilates and yoga, Danny Grealish was a troubled man who had been keeping a dark secret since he was eighteen years of age.

When he was younger Danny liked to play poker and he regularly went to poker schools at various North London establishments. One night he got in a game with six others in a rundown snooker club in Camden Town. Danny was good, he was two and a half grand up when it got to the last hand of the night. There were just two of the six men left, around £4,000 on the table and Danny was holding four queens.

Sat opposite Danny, holding his cards in one hand, was Terry Molloy, the middle brother of the North London crime family. Danny was gonna back his four queens, and why wouldn't he? Gradually, Danny's two and a half grand went on to the table as the stakes got raised and he was now playing on credit. Credit to anyone was bad, but credit to one of the most notorious loan sharks in North London was beyond bad. As the thousands went in Danny looked into Terry's eyes. *He can't be holding more than a box of queens?* After about half an hour there was over £21,000 on the table and a credit note for £15,000 from Danny to Terry Molloy. Then Molloy said, "Okay, I'll see you. What you got, kid?"

There was an intake of breath all round when Danny, confidently, turned over his four queens. Molloy looked at them, stunned, then looked into the eyes of the three others that had stayed to watch this match between the two best players there. Then, as he turned his hand over, he looked straight into Danny's eyes and smiled.

Cala de Mijas, two months earlier...

Kim got the fright of her life when she opened the door and saw the face of what she always thought was the love of her life standing there with a sheepish smile and a rucksack containing all his worldly belongings. "How's it going?" he asked.

"What the fuck? Joe?"

Joe explained to Kim what had happened and why he had to disappear. "Fuck, I never knew that about Danny. You know me and Karen don't talk, right?"

"Yeah, she told me. Shame that, she's your sister, your twin fucking sister."

"Yeah, well she backed that womanising old man of ours against mum, so she can fucking talk to him." It was Kim's "womanising old man" that had told Billy Dunne where Kim and her mum were living.

Billy and Jim Moore used to go greyhound racing, they had even owned a couple of dogs together. Billy, like most people, knew that Joe still held a torch for Kim and used to wind him up about it, when Joe would be on his case about the Wallace fight.

"You're too stressed lately, Joe, get over to Spain for a few days, she's in Mijas, just down the beach from Olivia's Restaurant. You'll get free digs, a bit of sun and your leg over at the same time."

"Just get me the Wallace fight, Billy, and shut the fuck up." It was a good light-hearted way to stop Joe pestering Billy about the fight, a fight that Billy couldn't deliver.

"Yeah, you can stay here for a bit, Joe, but I don't want no trouble coming to the door." As she was talking Joe saw a small boy walk over and stand behind his mother's legs looking up at him. "Elijah, this is Joe. Joe, this is Elijah. Joe's a friend of the family and he's going to be staying with us for a little while, Elijah. Okay?" The boy looked up at his mum clutching a stuffed bunny to his chest and nodded.

Joe looked at Kim. If anything she was even prettier than he had remembered from back in London, tanned with long, honey-brown hair and beautiful blues eyes. "I'd heard from Karen about the boy," Joe motioned towards the room that Elijah had gone into.

"Yeah, his dad didn't hang around long once he found out about the baby. He's back in Manchester or somewhere up north now. Glad really, he was a boxer as well, but he wasn't you, Joe."

Fourteen years earlier...

When Terry Molloy laid his cards face up on the table Danny had to look at them hard. It took a while for it to compute. There were no picture cards and they were all low numbers, all the cards were black digits on a white background, all the cards were clubs. *A flush, that's okay, a flush doesn't beat four of a kind.* He looked again: the 5, 4, 8, 7 and 6 of clubs. *A flush, that's good isn't it?* Then Terry rearranged the cards 4, 5, 6, 7, 8 of clubs. *That's not a flush, it's a running fucking flush! Fuck, fuck, fuck!*

Terry Molloy grinned as his arms circled around the pile of cash on the table as he drew it towards him, then he pulled out the credit note from the centre of his winnings and held it up so that Danny could read his own writing:

I owe £15,000 – Danny Grealish

Molloy looked at Danny. "I'll be in touch in the next few days about picking the money up." Then the villain turned around scooping the surplus cash into his pockets and walked out of the door.

Cala de Mijas...

It was going well with Kim and Joe got on well with Elijah. He was a nice, well-mannered kid and his mum had done a great job bringing him up on her own. Kim couldn't rely on her mum for help as due to her rapidly increasing dementia she had to be admitted to a care home around a mile away, where she needed the full-time care that Kim, with Elijah to look after and a part-time job teaching English, couldn't give her.

Joe liked Mijas, it was a nice town. They lived in a charming, butterscotch-coloured apartment with a balcony in Calle Butiplaya, a pretty little row of apartments right on Mijas beach. The people were friendly and it had nice bars and restaurants. In the mornings before it got too hot he'd go for long runs on the concrete pathway that ran along the beautiful sandy beach, the concrete turning into wooden decking as you climbed up past El Oceano Hotel towards Marbella. There was also some outdoor gym kit on the beach and if he got there early enough he'd have it to himself. He couldn't do any boxing though as he didn't want to give his identity away. He knew he was a wanted man and there would be a price on his head in the underworld. He was confident though that having shaved his head, grown a bleached blonde goatee beard and with clear lens, black-rimmed glasses he wouldn't be recognised by any of the ex-pats that frequented the area. Joe also gave himself a new name as Kim and her son were the only people that knew he was there. Kim's mum was struggling to remember who Kim was now, so there was little point in telling her and confusing her even more. Joe gave himself his uncle's first name coupled with his mother's maiden name. While he was in Spain Joe was Micky Clarke.

He got himself a job behind the bar at Biddy Mulligan's, the big Irish bar on the main street of Mijas. It was a lively sports pub and he enjoyed the banter with the clientele that got in there, a mixture of holidaymakers and local residents. He got on with everyone and, through one of the locals, he got a load of electrical work for one of the big property developers in the area. There were loads of villas being built around the golf courses in Mijas, and they all needed wiring and CCTV installing. It was a really good earner for Joe, all cash in hand, and he was snowed under with the work on the villas so he didn't really need the bar work, but he enjoyed the craic of Biddy Mulligan's.

It was from behind the bar in Biddy's that Joe watched George Wallace dismantle the brave but outclassed Italian journeyman Bruno Rossi on the wide screen TV that dominated the room. He had to stay silent as he heard the local opinions on the battle.

"Shame that Joe Fitzpatrick pulled out."

"Yeah, I heard he bottled it. Wallace is a different level."

"I don't know, Fitzpatrick's all wrong for him. Wallace doesn't like southpaws."

"I heard that Fitzpatrick's got a big problem with gear and he failed a drug test, that's why he's gone off the radar."

"Well let's hope it does happen one day, but you know what the fight game's like, it's all controlled by money. It'll probably never happen."

"Mad how he pulled out so late though. They said he got a cut in sparring, you don't do serious sparring so close to a fight, not a fight like that anyway. All sounds a bit dodge to me. Don't like that Marc Harris though, with his monopoly on the fighters he's ruining boxing."

It was hard for Joe to listen to the opinions of the room, some informed and others not. He thought of what might have been, how his life could have been so much different if only he hadn't got involved in Danny Grealish's problem with Tommy Molloy.

His mind wandered back to the day they were only eighteen years old when he, literally, had to hold a sobbing Danny up at his old man, Davy's, funeral. Then he thought of the day he had gone to see Danny at Om Squad, his ankle in so much pain that it was hard for him to walk. He was about to go into the building when he noticed Sean Molloy's trademark blue Bentley sat outside the vegan restaurant. His immediate concern was for Danny's welfare. Had Sean gone to put the frighteners on Danny because he wouldn't pay Tommy? No, he wouldn't get involved in something as menial as one of Tommy's minor protection jobs. It must be to do with Joe and Danny's friendship.

Joe had limped across the road to the cafe opposite, waiting, watching the entrance to Om Squad. How would it play out? If Danny was to be walked out by Sean Molloy and his men and bundled into the Bentley Joe would have to get involved. It was Joe they wanted, not Danny, he'd have to show himself and wait for the attack that would ensue. If Sean was on his own Joe, even with his twisted ankle, thought he would have a chance, but if there were more than just Sean there, or if Sean was "carrying" then Joe was in trouble. Seven or eight women had walked in and out of there in the time that Joe was watching the place, nearly all of them with a rolled-up yoga mat under their arm. The irony, he thought, these champions of peace and tranquillity are worshipping at what could be, in a few minutes time, the venue for some horrific violence.

Sean Molloy appeared walking out of the doors. He seemed to be on his own. *Result,* thought Joe. But where was Danny? Even from across the road Joe could see the damage his fists had inflicted on Molloy's ruggedly handsome features. *Fuck me, I caught him good,* thought Joe. Still no sign of Danny. Had Molloy beaten him up in there or threatened him? Joe went to get off his seat to go across the road but then Danny appeared looking in surprisingly good spirits. The pair shook hands, chatted a little more and then embraced before Sean walked over to his car and got in. Joe stared, gobsmacked, as this unbelievable scene played out in front of him. *What the fuck's going on?*

Fourteen years earlier...

It was two days after the card game, that card game, and Danny was serving customers in his mum and dad's cafe, Rosa's. As always there was a queue. Danny's mum made the best lasagne to take away and there was always queues at lunchtime from the locals for her Italian grub, proper hearty food.

"Lasagne to take away? Of course, how about some mozzarella with that? No, you're on a diet, love? I wondered why I was seeing less and less of you." Danny was on a roll with the customers and they loved him.

"Yes, sir? No food today, only a coffee? Of course, sir, I expect you got a bowl of soup with that haircut?" The customers laughed, but not all of them. Standing at the back of the cafe staring at Danny was Tommy Molloy, the youngest of the Molloy brothers. Danny knew him from school, he was a couple of years older and hung around with a different crowd to Danny and Joe. Danny's heart sank when he saw him.

"Mum, can you take over for five minutes? I've just got to pop out." Rosa came out of the kitchen.

"Yes, love, you okay?"

"Yeah, fine, I'll be back in five." Rosa watched as Danny walked over to Tommy Molloy, then they both left the cafe.

"Nice little business this," Tommy said to Danny. "Must take a few quid?" Danny looked at him.

"I haven't got the money, Tommy. What happens now?"

"Hang on, it's not your turn to speak yet and I haven't asked you anything. It's my turn to speak now, so where's Terry's fifteen grand?"

"I... I haven't got it, Tommy. I can get you some of it by the weekend." Tommy shook his head.

"How much of it?"

"I dunno, maybe seven or eight hundred quid?" Tommy looked at him and smiled patronisingly.

"Are you fucking winding me up? Are you? This isn't a fucking loan! This is legitimate money you owe Terry!"

Danny looked back at him. In a straightener Danny thought he could do Tommy, but Tommy was a bully and knew that Danny wouldn't dare lay a finger on him because of what he had behind him, who he had behind him.

"No, it's not a wind-up, it's all I can get hold of." Tommy looked over Danny's shoulder at Rosa's cafe.

"How much does this place take a week?"

"Dunno, sometimes more than others."

"How fucking much?"

"Last week twenty-one grand, the week before twenty-two and a half. It goes up and down." Molloy looked deep in thought. *Don't like where this is going,* thought Danny.

"Come and see me and Terry at six tonight in The Nelson."

Danny knew The Lord Nelson, it was a rough house pub just off Kilburn High Road and was the main hangout of the Molloys. Tommy Molloy turned away before Danny could even react and walked off down the street, pulling a packet of fags out of his inside pocket as he did so. *This wasn't good.*

Rosa came out of the cafe. "What did he want, Danny? Why are you talking with them?"

"Leave it, Mum, it's nothing, just something I need to sort out."

"Thanks anyway, Danny, but I don't think there's anything I could eat off there to be honest." Frankie Dunne smiled as he looked at Om Squad's extensive vegan menu. "I don't even know what half of these fucking things are. What's jackfruit? Fucks sake, Dan, I struggled with oven chips when they came out, but some of these fucking things..." Frank slid the menu back across the table to Danny.

"I haven't heard from him, Frank, not at all. It's weird." Danny looked across at the wise old boxing trainer.

"I'd have thought you'd be the first bloke he'd get in touch with," said Frank, "unless he thinks he'd be putting heat on you by getting in touch? If you don't know anything you can't say nothing, then you can't be under pressure. Like he's protecting you? I dunno, something don't add up."

They sat there thinking, then after three or four minutes of silence Frank's eyes widened and he sat up. "How's your missus' sister? What's her name again?"

"Kim," said Danny. "We haven't heard from her for a while, her and Karen fell out when their mum caught Jim at it with one of the barmaids at the dog track, so her mum fucked off to Spain and Kim went with her. He's a useless fucker."

"It may not be anything," said Frank, "but Billy used to wind Joe up all the time about going out to see her in Spain," said Frank. "Any idea whereabouts she is in Spain, Dan?"

"Yeah, I know where she is, but no, he wouldn't be there, Frank. I'm sure he told me he wasn't interested in Kim no more now she's got that kid," said Danny.

Frank sat there looking down at the table made from twisted salvaged timber then got up to leave. "If you hear anything, Danny, give me a shout. You know he's like a

39

son to me and fuck I'm worried for the kid. This ain't gonna end good, I can't see it ending good for Joe at all."

That's where he is, Mijas, thought Danny.

Frank scraped his thinning hair back over his forehead with the palm of his right hand, more out of stress than grooming, and got up to go, shaking his head, without making any kind of dent in Om Squad's bountiful larder of grains and plant based produce.

"Fucking jackfruit, what's that all about?" he muttered to himself as he left. Then Danny took his mobile out of his inside pocket and rang Sean Molloy.

Fourteen years earlier...

Danny was nervous as he pushed open the door of The Lord Nelson pub. The Nelson was looking "tired", it had not had a lick of paint for over ten years and was painted moss green and white on the outside, the white having yellowed over the years. He shoved through the heavy dark wood door with its etched frosted glass panel. Inside it was gloomy but light enough to see clearly, but the nicotine stained woodwork and artexed ceiling with maroon and white striped walls made it feel much smaller than it actually was.

This was a different Lord Nelson than the one Joe Fitzpatrick would walk into fourteen years later for that fateful meeting with Sean Molloy. The Lord Nelson that Joe had leapt out of the window to escape from had benefitted from over half a million pounds worth of refurbishment being spent on it, bringing it up to date, turning it into a lively profitable gastropub in the evenings that even had a vegan menu, and with the added benefit of laundering a huge amount of money in the process of the renovation works.

There were seven or eight of the Molloys' heavies stood around the bar when Dan walked in. The place smelled of fags, stale beer and puff.

"Who are you?" a large dark-haired man who looked like he was about to explode out of his tight shirt barked in an Eastern European accent.

"I've got a meeting with Tommy and Terry," said Dan nervously.

These were big men, big, steroid affected men challenging an eighteen year old fit but scrawny kid. The man motioned towards a door at the back of the bar with his eyes. "Up the stairs." Dan felt every pair of eyes on him as he crossed the room and pushed against the door.

He walked up the creaking stairs and pulled the handle down on the door at the top. It opened up to a large room with one desk on the left-hand side. Behind the desk sat Sean Molloy, the oldest of the Molloy brothers and head of their criminal operation.

"Sit down!" Molloy barked at Danny.

"I've got a meeting with Tommy and, er, Terry," stuttered Dan.

"No you ain't, I've bought Terry's debt so now you owe me. Now where's the money?"

Dan looked down at the desk he was sat at. *Jesus, I'll never, ever pick up another playing card,* he thought.

"You ain't got it, have you?" Sean looked at Dan as he shook his head. "Well I'm not a fucking charity so I've got a solution to help you out." Danny looked up. "What I'm gonna do, son," said Molloy, "is pass that debt on." Danny sat there looking helpless. His fate was going to be decided for him by this North London gangster. *Help me out? What the fuck?*

"You don't owe me fifteen grand anymore." Danny knew that this was no benevolent gesture going to be shown by the head of North London's notorious crime family towards a naive, cocky eighteen year old that had got in over his head at the wrong card school. "No, you don't owe me that dough anymore, you haven't got it anyway, so that debt has been passed on to your old man's cafe. Rosa's now owes me fifteen grand and I want it back."

"But it's got nothing to do with the cafe," Dan protested. "It's my debt, not my old man's."

"Shut up and listen, you cunt!" Molloy barked at Danny. "I'm gonna take one week's takings from that cafe as settlement for your debt or I'll take the café. I've always wanted to get into that game and Tommy says you're good at that game. Says you're a natural with the punters." Molloy stared at Dan. "That's the deal."

"You can't," said Danny, looking over at Sean. Danny hated the fact that his eyes were welling up as he tried to bargain with Molloy. "They ain't done nothing," he pleaded. "They don't even know I play cards." Sean stood up and stooped over Dan.

"Not my fucking problem, son. That's the deal and this is how it's going to play out."

Cala de Mijas...

"I'm going back to London for a while, Kim." Joe looked across at her as he threw some bits into a large rucksack.

"Do you think that's wise, Joe? Don't you want to lay low over here?"

"I've got to go for a bit, Kim, got to sort this shit out."

Joe had been in Mijas for nearly six months now. He had kept himself fit, the ankle felt good and he had got a load of dough together from his electrician work that paid really well, and was going to have a few days in London staying somewhere far away from Kilburn.

Malaga Airport was quiet when Joe got there. It was out of season and there were not too many passengers that morning, which was handy as Joe's gate number for the 11.10 Ryanair flight to Stansted was already flashing on the screens when he arrived. He got through customs, waited patiently in the "Any Other Passengers" queue then boarded the plane, sat down and got his latest novel out.

Joe liked William Boyd's books and *Any Human Heart* was a particular favourite. Basically, it was a chronological history of anything and anyone relevant in the twentieth century. He was halfway through another Boyd tome *Ordinary Thunderstorms* and expected to finish it on the flight. It was, ironically, about a wanted man on the run fearing for his life and hiding out in London.

While Joe had been hurriedly sorting his boarding pass and passport out for customs, he never noticed the two huge men thirty metres to his left coming through arrivals and heading towards the taxi rank.

As the plane took off Joe had to keep rereading pages of his book as he wasn't really taking it in, his mind was on Sean Molloy and how to get at him.

"Any drinks for you, sir?" Joe looked up to see a blue suited steward looking down at him.

Glancing at the name badge, Joe replied, "Can I get a black coffee please, Dennis."

"Yes, of course. Would you like any chocolate bar for half price with your hot drink?"

"No thanks, just the coffee."

"Any scratchcards for you today, sir?"

"No thanks, just the coffee's great."

"Okay," said Dennis, pouring the coffee and giving Joe a frosty look. "And would you be interested in signing up for a Ryanair credit card today, with a special offer of a two-week interest free window?"

"No, Dennis," Joe snapped, "I just want a fucking coffee!"

Dennis paused for a bit, then said, "Okay, calm down, sir, take a deep breath and then maybe hold it in for about an hour."

Joe sat there shaking his head as Dennis turned on his heels and minced away in triumph. As he sipped on his hard-earned black coffee Joe discarded the book – not Boyd's best work – and thought about that day in Molloy's office when the gangster had tried to stroke his cheek. There had been rumours about Sean Molloy for years, never substantiated, but no one would dare question him about them, so for now they were just rumours. This was Joe's target. He was going into the rumour business.

Fourteen years earlier...

"When does the banking get done?" Sean snarled at Danny.

"Friday mornings. The old man cashes up on Thursday evening, leaves it in the safe overnight and goes to the bank first thing on Friday. He won't let anyone else do the banking." Dan was staring down at the table as he spoke.

"Okay, I'll have some boys waiting outside first thing on Friday to interrupt that little arrangement. I don't need to tell you that if you bubble this up to anyone your life ain't worth shit and we'll burn the place down anyway."

"Wait," Danny said, "I've got a key and I know the code to the safe. I could let your blokes in on Thursday night and open the safe for them." Danny, understandably, was worried that his old man, who was a feisty little Cork man, would put up a struggle and get hurt. "They could make it look like a burglary."

Sean sat back and stared at him. "Okay, meet my boys here at ten o'clock on Thursday night. Now fuck off out of here."

Danny got up but he was in a daze. *What the fuck have I committed to?* At least this way his old man wouldn't get hurt, not physically anyway. It seemed little consolation to him now though. What the fuck had he done?

Cala de Mijas...

Kim dropped Elijah off at his playgroup on her way to see her mum in the care home. "See you later, little fella," she said as she gave him a kiss. "We'll have a nice tea tonight, just you and me again." Elijah ran into the whitewashed building full of kids his own age, clutching his favourite little stuffed bunny under his arm.

Across the road in a hire car two men watched as Kim got into her white and black four-seater Smart car and headed up the mountain towards Mijas town.

******

Alek Nowak had left Krakow twenty years earlier when he was seventeen. The victim of an abusive stepfather, he was forced to leave when after a particularly drunken night his stepfather started beating his mother. Alek came home from training to see him pulling his mother around by her hair. Alek, in a fit of rage, beat the drunk to death and left Poland that night, never to see his mother again. He went to Dublin first working in the booming building industry over

45

there, but when the Celtic Tiger collapsed and the work dried up he crossed the Irish Sea to seek work in London.

From the age of eight Alek had practised Krav Maga, the martial art that was founded by the Israeli Army and was able to continue it when in Dublin and London through different schools. After his recent grading he was now a black belt 7th Dan which made it hard to get him fights as this was an elite level, so he took to boxing in order to get the fights that his Krav Maga prowess prevented him from having. Although lacking in prowess under the Queensberry rules, Alek Nowak still made some decent undercards and won more fights than he lost in a fighting discipline that was not, by any means, his forte.

As he went from job to job Alek soon found out that London was not exactly paved with gold at that time either and spent most of his days standing with a mix of other Eastern Europeans at the car park of The Crown in Cricklewood from five in the morning hoping for a builder's van to pull up and offer him "a start", which meant a day's work. Invariably if a van did pull up Alek would be picked out from the others for that day's gig because of his stature. Most of the days though a van wouldn't pull up at all and he would be left standing there for the entire day.

It was on one of these seemingly fruitless days that a blue Bentley pulled up and a man that Alek later found out to be Sean Molloy got out. Alek thought he must be going into the pub as it was one o'clock in the afternoon and, despite there being a recession going on, the Irish in the area usually found the means to "go down to the corner for a jar". Alek never joined them as he didn't touch a drop of alcohol, his experiences with his stepfather told him everything he needed to know about the stuff.

"Are you Alek?" Sean Molloy looked down at the large man sitting on the wall.

"Who is asking?" said Alek.

"I may have some work for you," said Molloy.

Sean Molloy was always on the lookout for top, local muscle as he tried to build up a select crew to protect and expand his firm's empire of greed, violence, drugs and profit. He had his ear to the ground in most of the local gyms and clubs, hence his active pursuit of Joe Fitzpatrick, and had heard about this Pole that was making a name for himself at "Hand to Hand" Krav Maga school in Willesden.

That fruitful meeting for Alek resulted in him now, eleven years later, being one of the Molloys' top boys.

Craig Connor had come down to London from Sauchiehall Street, Glasgow, ironically only one street away from Berkeley Street where George Wallace had grown up. Connor's father was looking for work so he upped sticks and took his ten year old boy down to stay with his brother's family in Farrant Avenue, Wood Green, North London. The relocation was as much to look for work as to get away from his wife and three other kids, all girls, and the responsibility of payments that in his words were "holding him back".

The old man struggled to find work though, and most days he would be found propping up the bar in The Nightingale pub down the road from Farrant Avenue, and when the money or credit ran out he would stagger home and take his misinterpreted misfortune out violently on his only son.

Wood Green at that time was a melting pot of Asian, black, Irish and overzealous English patriots. It was a harsh area for a ten year old "Jock" to move into and Craig soon learned to be handy with his fists, which developed into minor crime then on to armed robbery, and eventually he ended up doing seven years inside for manslaughter.

It was while he was doing this sentence that he was diagnosed as a sociopath and the reason given was that he was "a victim of his circumstances".

Craig Connor never stood a chance. The manslaughter charge should have been murder, but because he was working for the Molloys when it happened he had the advantage of their top solicitor and a judge that was very much in their pocket. His silence, before and during his sentence, was rewarded by being given a permanent job with the crime family on his release.

He had used his time in prison purposefully though, gaining himself an O Level in Spanish and a black belt in tae kwon do.

And now this unlikely Polish-Scottish duo found themselves sitting in a hired silver Audi opposite a crèche in the pretty Spanish town of Cala de Mijas on what Sean Molloy had described to them as "a mini holiday".

Fourteen years earlier...

Danny was getting ready to leave work at six. "What you doing tonight, Danny?" Davy Grealish asked as he looked up at his son. Danny was taller than the old man now.

"Not much, Dad," Danny replied. "Probably gonna meet Joe for a couple of games of snooker."

"Well you give him my best, son, he's a good lad is Joe. You're lucky to have a friend like him, but make sure you kick his arse on the snooker table," Davy laughed. Danny couldn't look at his old man as he left. What the fuck had he done?

At five to ten that night Danny walked into The Lord Nelson and met up with Sean Molloy and one of his henchmen.

"Thought I'd come along on this one," Sean said. "Stops any of the takings going astray. Sometimes you leave a cash job to others and it doesn't all filter back, if you know what

I mean? Mind you, if all the money came back untouched, every penny, I'd be even more suspicious of the blokes that carried it out."

The henchman dropped Sean and Danny off round the corner from Rosa's and sat in the car to wait for their return. The two men made their way to the front where Danny, with shaking hands, unlocked the Yale lock. The muted bleep of the alarm system kicked in as soon as the door opened and Danny went to the white box inside the cupboard by the serving hatch and punched in 2-0-0-2, 20th of February, the date of Danny's birth and in Davy's own words, "The happiest day of my life."

The two men walked through the serving area and out to the back of the cafe where behind four rows of stacked chairs there was a floor to ceiling cupboard. Danny just wanted this over now, so he nervously opened the cupboard to reveal a small safe built into the wall. He keyed the number combination in, 1-6-0-8, 16th of August, Davy and Rosa's wedding anniversary, and the steel door jerked open.

Bermondsey...

Joe left Liverpool Street at the Bishopsgate exit and headed down towards London Bridge. It was a nice day so he thought he'd walk. Joe had booked an Airbnb in Snowsfields just off Bermondsey Street by London Bridge. He knew the area well as he had sparred a few times at Rooney's Gym under the arches on Holyrood Street which backed on to Bermondsey Street. He liked it round there, it had an almost village-like feel and, more importantly, being

South East London it was well away from the North West London of Kilburn and the Molloys.

He walked over London Bridge and turned left into Tooley Street, then right after a couple of hundred yards on to Bermondsey Street. He smiled as he walked past what used to be the back entrance to Rooney's Gym; the gym had been closed down for a while due to the redevelopment of London Bridge Station. *Shame that was a great little gym.* He then turned right as he came out of the tunnel and on to Snowsfields and found the apartment opposite The Horseshoe pub.

He punched in the code that he had been sent by the landlord of the flat and opened the key lock to reveal a set of keys.

Number 24 was a nice apartment on the ground floor with a partial view of The Shard, and it was to be his home for a while until he got things sorted. The landlord had left a few beers in the fridge as a welcoming present and a note with the Wi-Fi code and a list of things to do in the area.

So, as well as a host of good bars and restaurants that were on the landlord's list, he could go aboard HMS Belfast, get lashed on the Bermondsey beer mile, try and work out the contemporary art at the the White Cube Gallery, test his head for heights at the top of The Shard, or he could go to Borough Market and pay an absolute fortune for a blood orange.

Fourteen years earlier...

"Don't go tonight, Davy, go in the morning." Rosa Grealish linked arms with her husband as they left Beacon Bingo Club in Cricklewood, the shrink wrapped, colourful fruit bowl under Davy's other arm being testament to a modestly successful evening.

"No, I want to get it out of the way. I've got a bread delivery at six in the morning and if I don't do it now it won't get done. I won't be long."

"Okay, well I'll get the kettle on and see you back at the house." Davy handed Rosa the fruit bowl and headed towards the cafe.

Davy could kick himself for not leaving the bins out for the next morning's collection, but if he did it now he wouldn't have to be there before them at 5am the next day as that was their usual collection time at Rosa's. This way he could nick another hour in bed and get there just before the bread delivery.

Cala de Mijas

Bridget Moore sat there while her daughter Kim told her all about Elijah's school, how he got on great with all the other children and how much he was enjoying it. Then Kim's mobile rang. Kim looked at the number flashing on the phone.

"Talk of the devil, Mum, that's the school on the phone now." Kim may as well have been talking to herself as Bridget just stared out of the window into space. Kim knew that not much was getting through to her mum, she was used to it as her condition deteriorated, but now and again a word or two would register and Bridget's eyes would widen and sparkle and that made it all worthwhile for Kim. "The devil?" Bridget muttered.

Kim stuttered on the phone. "What? What men? Who?" She tried to make sense of the broken English with a Spanish accent coming over the phone.

"One madder, she saw two men outside the *escuela* so we call *policia*. When *policia* come the men go away. We are telling all madders to peek up their child today for the safferty."

Fourteen years earlier…

Davy knew there was something up when he got to Rosa's. The door was locked but when he instinctively went to key in the alarm code after opening it there was no bleep. The alarm hadn't been set. Okay, so he forgot the bins, but he would never forget to set the alarm. *Unless I'm finally going senile*, he thought to himself. As he walked through he heard voices and rustling noises coming from the back storeroom where the safe was. Davy wasn't a big man but anyone that knew him was wary of his Irish temper. He stood bolt still. *Have they heard me?* No, he didn't think so, as they seemed to carry on muttering and doing whatever it was that created the rustling.

As Davy eased his way behind the counter and into the kitchen he could see torchlight coming from the storeroom and movement. It looked like two men. It was dark and there were four sets of chairs stacked at the door to the room so he could only make out shadows, but they were emptying the contents of his safe into what looked like a sports bag. He leaned over the stainless steel worktop in the kitchen and picked up a black handled chef's knife, edged towards the chairs and then burst through them.

"Fucking rob me will you?" he shouted at the startled man loading the sports bag.

As he lunged to stab the man the other robber appeared from his left and, seeing what was about to happen, shouted, "No, Dad!" instinctively shoving his father back away from Molloy and stopping him from stabbing the robber.

Davy Grealish turned his head mid-fall after hearing his only child's voice shout at him, and with a quizzical look at Danny he fell into the nearest stack of chairs, collapsing face down on top of the hand holding the chef's knife which was upturned, half of it buried in Davy Grealish's chest. This was the dark secret that Danny had been harbouring for fourteen years, the darkest of all secrets. He had killed his old man and the only other person that knew it was Sean Molloy.

St John's Wood...

Joe pulled up on the scooter that he had hired from a company in Clerkenwell Road which he'd paid £250 for five days including insurance. It was a good way to get around. He had a large Sturm & Drang messenger bag that Amazon had delivered to the flat in Spain draped across his body, and with a full face crash helmet for anonymity he blended into the background as just another motorcycle courier among the hundreds of others going about their business in the metropolis.

Joe was parked up in leafy Hamilton Terrace in St John's Wood. The properties here were enormous displays of affluence and he was sat opposite a large yellow brick, semi-detached Victorian terrace house arranged over four floors. Despite the hefty price tags on the residences in this prestigious tree-lined boulevard, none of the properties had very large drives. The yellow house that Joe was sat opposite only had space for maybe two normal size cars or just one car if it was the large blue Bentley that currently filled the space.

So this is where the fuckpig lives.

Joe had heard Molloy lived near Danny's new house and the car gave the location up. He stared at the house for a couple of minutes, checking the security arrangements and any cameras on the street, then fired up the scooter to drive the short distance to Kilburn High Road.

Kilburn...

Rosa never returned to the cafe that was named after her. She was heartbroken as she had lost her "shining light" the day that Davy was murdered. Danny took Rosa's cafe over and inherited a "silent partner" in Sean Molloy.

"It's 25% of everything or, well, you don't want people to know what you did, do you? Your poor mum will be so upset if she thought you'd killed your own dad."

So that was Danny's lot, beholden to Sean Molloy for the foreseeable all because of a game of cards.

******

Business was booming at the cafe. Rosa still cooked her popular lasagne from home and Danny brought batches of it in every day, as well as adding other vegetarian and vegan lunch options which went down a storm with their increasingly "wellness aware" customers.

As an experiment Danny got Rosa to replace the beef with some mixed vegetables making it a vegetarian lasagne and, much to Rosa's displeasure, it soon started outselling the meat version. It crossed his mind but Danny didn't have the heart or balls to ask Rosa to replace the mozzarella with a dairy free cheese alternative, turning it into a vegan lasagne. If he had asked she'd have probably clumped him with a ladle as replacing the meat was sacrilege enough.

The cafe's twice weekly meat order was getting smaller and smaller, so much so that Kevin, the owner of "Pleased To Meat You", the huge butcher shop in Cricklewood that supplied all Rosa's meat, called in to see Danny.

"I don't get it, Dan, if they hate meat so much why do these bleeding vegans dress their food up to look like meat? It's like lesbians that use a dildo. They made their fucking choice."

Danny smiled at the analogy.

"It's just the way things are going these days, Kev. People want to try different things. You never know, meat will probably be back in fashion next month." Dan didn't believe his own statement but could see Kevin was worried about the outlook for his business and other such traditional establishments.

"Going well here though, mate. Looks like you're outgrowing this gaff," said Kevin.

"Yeah, funny you should say that, Kev, I've been thinking of looking at somewhere bigger. Also, with what happened to the old man and all that Mum won't come back in here and it would be nice to have her back in helping out now and again. She likes the banter with the customers and it would take her mind off the old man for a bit."

"Yeah, that was a fucker. Sorry, Dan, I thought the world of Davy, he was my first big customer when I got going, helped me out no end. They never did get the cunts that did it, did they?"

"No, mate, and they've closed the case now."

"Well even if they pretend they don't know who did it, we all know it was them cunts that I have to hand over a monkey a week to, that's probably what it was about if you ask me. Davy said they'd been on to him a couple of times about giving them dough but he refused. Tough little fucker the old man was, Dan."

Danny just stared at the black and white tiled floor, his thoughts wandering to that fateful night and what happened just five yards from where he was sitting with Kevin.

"Sorry, Dan, I didn't mean to go on about it. It must upset you."

"Yeah it does, Kev, but we've just got to try and get on with it."

"Anyway, if you do find somewhere bigger, Dan, let me know 'cos I'd probably be interested in this gaff, what with all you salad munchers about. I could do with a slightly smaller place than I'm in now and something this size would do nicely," Kevin said, looking around the shop.

******

"Well I'll still want a monkey a week off him. Don't care if his business is going shit," Sean said staring at Danny.

"I don't think that's a problem, Sean. Kevin could move in to where we are now. His overheads will come down, so if anything he'll have more chance of finding your dough every week. You never know, you may be able to nick another long 'un out of him and hopefully we can find a bigger gaff for the new vegan place, somewhere local."

Danny Grealish was embracing this lifestyle. He knew that Sean had a lot of commercial properties, mainly bars and restaurants, scattered around North West London, as well as a gentlemen's club "Libretto" in Greek Street, Soho. All of these were "acquired" through bad debt where the owners had ended up reneging on payments to the Molloys.

Danny had only been to Libretto once to drop some money off to Sean. It was an old-fashioned, very exclusive gentlemen's club known for its discretion and complete press and mobile phone ban. Members handed their phones in at reception. There was only ever one instance where a member had their membership rescinded for leaking stories from within the club. It was full of dark wood and buttoned, oxblood-coloured leather, and there were usually two or three well-known figures from stage, screen or the establishment to be found using the club at any time, as their privacy was guaranteed in Libretto which was a big draw.

"Yeah, that makes sense I suppose, Dan. Tell you what I have got, there's a Turkish down the Edgware Road that owes me a load of dough. I could sling them out, tosh it up a bit and you could put your veggie place in there. Gonna mean my cut goes up to 35% though."

Danny had earlier explained his new vegan restaurant and yoga retreat idea to Sean. "So it'll be a restaurant with no fucking meat?"

"Yeah, it's vegan, Sean, it's a restaurant where they don't eat meat. Everyone's going mad for it, you'll understand when you see the numbers, believe me."

"Sounds like a load of old bollocks to me, but what the fuck do I know?"

Frankie Dunn was "doing a bit" while the gym was empty, having a workout on the heavy bag when a voice came from behind him at the back of the building. "Still got it then?"

Frank stopped hitting the big bag and without turning around replied, "Where the fuck have you been, Joe?" He turned to face him. "And what the fuck's happened to your barnet? I'd have walked straight past you in the street. You look like a right ponce with that silly little beard and glasses, and you've put on a bit of timber. You're probably a light heavyweight now. I told you that's your proper weight."

"Well, I haven't got a fight to train for at the moment, Frank, not in the ring anyway."

Frank looked at Joe, shook his head and said, "I'll get the kettle on, son, and you can tell me what the fuck's going on."

Frank shut and bolted the front door of the gym. Only Joe knew the way in through the rear of the building, it was over a wall and in through the toilet window which never used to shut properly. Joe had been used to getting in that way since he was a teenager when he used to sneak in to train whenever the gym was shut. Joe never thought Frankie knew about this but you can't pull the wool over someone like Frankie Dunne's eyes, and Frank used to "accidentally" leave fresh towels out so Joe could use the freezing showers afterwards.

"You shouldn't have come back, Joe, he's serious."

"Well so am I, Frank, he's cost me everything and he's not getting away with it. For too long people round here have been letting that lot get away with murder, literally. Someone's got to stand up to them."

"But that man isn't you, Joe, you're a good kid, you don't need this. Just get the fuck away from here while you still can. Where have you been anyway?"

Joe explained to Frank how he had been holed up in Mijas with Kim.

"I said that to Danny and he said there was no way you'd go over there. He said you told him you'd gone off that bird since she had a kid with someone else."

"I never said anything like that to Dan. Why would he say that? There's something strange going on with Danny and the Molloys, Frank."

"What do you mean, son?"

"Don't know. I saw Sean Molloy at Danny's gaff in Edgware. You'd have thought by looking at them that they were the greatest of pals."

"Really? I'll see what I can find out, Joe. But stay away from Danny 'til I can find out something. They're crawling all over his gaff."

"Okay, Frank, but don't leave it too long as I want to go and ask him what the fuck's going on myself." Then after a pause Joe looked at Frank. "Frank, you told me once when you had a few whiskeys down you, one Christmas I think it was, why Sean Molloy suddenly left this club a few years ago."

"Did I? Fuck, I should learn to keep my mouth shut when I'm on the gargle," said the old trainer.

"Tell me about it again, Frank."

Bermondsey...

Joe was having a pint of Camden Hells in The Woolpack on Bermondsey Street. He was digesting the information he had found out earlier that day. Frank had confirmed what he had told him previously in a drunken rant about Molloy's sudden departure from St Anthony's Gym.

Joe looked around the pub at the punters. Bermondsey Street had changed since Joe had last trained there, and a lot of the character seemed to have gone from the area to be replaced by wealth. Small independent shops like "Cockfighter of Bermondsey" had been replaced by estate agents, and cafes had given way to fancy French restaurants and tapas bars. Rooney's Gym had been mown down to make way for the huge new London Bridge development. *Yeah,* thought Joe, *I suppose it's progress, but the place is in danger of disappearing up its own arse.*

Joe's phone rang and Kim's name flashed on the screen. "Hello, darling, you okay?" said Joe. He was answered by a screaming Kim.

"They're over here, Joe! They're fucking over here!" Joe went outside of the bar and tried to calm Kim down.

"Easy baby, take some deep breaths. Now tell me what's happened." Kim was sobbing uncontrollably.

"They're here, Joe, they're here."

"Who's there, Kim? Who?"

"Two men were parked outside Elijah's school this morning. They were there for a couple of hours and one of the mums noticed and reported them to the local police. When the police turned up they sped off. The police tried to trace the car but it had false plates on it. They're here, Joe, they're fucking here. I told you I didn't want this, I told you." She was in a state.

"Okay, calm down, Kim, and don't go back to the apartment. I'll get a flight back tonight. Have you got somewhere you can go?"

"Yes, yes, I grabbed a few bits from the flat and picked up Elijah. We're on our way to my friend's place in Benalmadena. She said I could stay there for a while."

"Okay, I'll get a flight back to—"

"No, Joe," Kim interrupted him. "Don't come back. You're bringing shit to our door. It's too dangerous you being around us. They were waiting outside Elijah's school for fuck's sake." Kim cut the call before Joe could reply. There was nothing he could do to talk her round, nothing.

And there was nothing he could do about the silver rented Audi four cars behind the black and white Smart car on the AP-7 road from Mijas to Benalmadena.

Cala de Mijas...

Alek Nowak and Craig Connor had been sat outside Escuela Infantile Buenbebe in Mijas for nearly three hours when the police car came round the corner. The plan had been to wait until Fitzpatrick's girl came to pick up the little boy, follow them, and then when they were off the main drag take the boy. In the ensuing car chase that followed the pair had easily shaken off the *policia*. The local law enforcement weren't used to dealing with criminals of the calibre of Nowak and Connor and definitely couldn't handle Nowak's prowess behind a steering wheel. They'd found the girl easy enough but were struggling with Joe. The bloke they were told she lived with didn't sound like him; they'd shown Fitzpatrick's photo around a few bars but no one had seen him, and they were told by a couple of people that the bloke she was living with was English but his name was Micky Clarke and he worked at Biddy Mulligan's but looked nothing like Joe Fitzpatrick.

The men went to Biddy Mulligan's the day after they got there but were told that Micky had gone to Dublin for a few days to catch up with some family, the lie that Joe had spun to Andy the owner of the bar.

"This Micky Clarke has gone to Dublin," Connor told Sean on the phone. "So we can't even tell if it's him or not."

"Well you ain't going on another holiday in fucking Dublin. Take the boy anyway, then he'll come to you and we'll find out if it's him," Sean replied.

******

Nowak and Connor got along okay. They had been put together by the Molloys once before on a job for Tommy Molloy that involved evicting an Indian family from their restaurant and home because they were late with their protection payments. So they kind of knew each other and had the sort of mutual respect that anyone would have when they know that the other person would kill them without question or remorse if ordered to.

Neither of the men slept very well in each other's company.

The journey over to Spain had been interesting. The pair of them sat boulder shoulder to boulder shoulder on a delayed Jet2 flight from Stansted, the slight girl shoe horned into the window seat next to them resisting the temptation to go to the toilet despite needing to and sat with her head buried in Jack Kerouac's *On The Road.* She was hoping to look invisible to the two shaven headed lumps to her right that were obviously, to all the passengers that saw them, not going on a beach holiday.

"Would you like a double bed or two singles?" asked the receptionist at the VIK Gran Hotel in Mijas to the two as they enquired about room availability.

"What the...?" Connor asked reddening.

"A double bed for you or two singles?" the girl asked again in broken English. She had seen enough gay couples checking in with the shaven headed muscular look that made this pair look stereotypical.

"Fuck off! I'm nae sleeping with this fucker," the Scotsman protested. "I want a separate room on the other side of the fucking hotel!"

Nowak just stared forward impassively, then said, "Don't kid yourself, Mister Scotsman, I wouldn't sleep with you anyway."

"Oh, I'm sorry." The receptionist blushed realising she had misread the situation. "I assumed you were here for the Twice Girls tonight."

"Who the fuck are the Twice Girls?" growled Connor.

"They're a Spice Girls tribute act that are on in the main lounge this evening. They're very popular, particulary among the local gay community," she replied.

"But why are they called the Twice Girls?" the Scotsman asked.

"Because there's only two of them."

Kilburn...

Joe parked the scooter on the other side of the road, fifty metres away from The Lord Nelson. He walked up and stood on the opposite side of the road to the pub looking at it while still wearing his crash helmet. Memories flashed back of that fateful day when he tumbled out of the window twisting his ankle, effectively ending his boxing career and, potentially, his life. His plan came to life when he saw Tommy Molloy walk out of the back doors and into the courtyard to light up a cigarette. *Touch!* thought Joe. *They do say smoking's bad for you, Tommy boy.*

Molloy never saw Joe until he was three or four metres away. Seeing a man purposefully walking towards him with a full face crash helmet on startled Tommy.

"Who the fuck?"

Joe landed a straight left hand flush on Tommy's cheek sending him flying back into a wall where Joe swung him round and wrapped his left arm around his throat, grabbing onto his own right shoulder then bringing his right arm up as he pushed the back of Molloy's head with the palm of his hand into the tightening vice-like squeeze of a rear naked choke. This way there would be no noise to alert any security.

Joe had about twenty seconds to get his message over to the youngest Molloy before he would pass out from lack of oxygen. He spat the words into Tommy's ear.

"You tell that cunt of a brother of yours that I'm over here now and I'm coming for him. If anything happens to that girl and her little boy in Spain Sean Molloy is a dead man."

Tommy Molloy's eyes were bulging, then he collapsed lifelessly into Joe's grip. Joe let him drop to the floor, unconscious, and returned to the scooter.

******

Terry Molloy could usually be found in "The Gaslight" pub about a mile down the road from The Lord Nelson. Terry, the middle of the three brothers, was the quietest but just as happy to be as violent a bully as the other pair. He was happy having a beer "out of the limelight", whereas Tommy and Sean were more gregarious and liked the adulation that came with owning successful businesses and mingling with the customers.

64

Tommy would always be in The Lord Nelson embracing the large numbers that now flocked to the revamped gastropub, whereas Sean would usually satisfy his ego in his West End club mixing with A-listers and members of the establishment that were always keen to be associated with the celebrity gangster.

Joe parked around the corner from The Gaslight and waited for the fallout. The jungle drums would soon start beating.

After a couple of minutes the front door to the pub flew open and Terry Molloy rushed out on his mobile shouting, "What do you mean?" He paused "Who fucking did it?" He looked up at the night sky. "Him? How? I thought he was in fucking Spain! I'll fucking burst that cunt! I'm on my way." He cut the phone call dead and put his phone in his jacket pocket.

"Come on then, burst me you fucking melt!" Terry turned round to see the crash helmeted figure in front of him. As Terry moved his hand to his inside pocket Joe was on him. A left hook was followed by a right liver punch which sucked all the breath from Molloy's body, dropping him to the floor and cracking two ribs in the process. "You tell your brother I'm here." Terry Molloy was on all fours, his forehead touching the pavement, gasping for air. "And if anything happens to that girl and her boy in Spain you're all getting it! That fucking clear?" Molloy groaned, still desperately gasping for air.

Soho...

Sean Molloy was in Libretto talking to a small select group about his latest property venture. He was broadening his empire by moving into South London. "So, the investment opportunities are huge, Camberwell Green is the gateway from The Elephant & Castle to Peckham Rye and it's still undiscovered. You can buy any of these apartments off plan for the square root of fuck all from Friday. It's buying money."

"But how are you able to knock down that huge magistrates' court and build on the land? That courthouse, why, it's been there for years," Kenneth Carmen asked.

Carmen was a well-respected food critic and in his day he owned a couple of Michelin star restaurants and was now to be found on Channel Four hosting *Easy as Pie*, the station's most popular cookery show. He was now in his late sixties and was also famous for "penning" a number of bestselling recipe books that were ghost written in his absence. He was way too fond of alcohol, Negronis being his current tipple of choice, and would regularly brag about his books. "The first time I read the books that I'm supposed to have fucking written is when they are already bestsellers! It's literally money for jam, dear boy!"

"How am I able to shut down that huge magistrates' court?" Molloy replied to the food critic. "Let's just say I've got friends in high places." Then he patted the man to his left on the shoulder.

The man to Molloy's left looked uneasy about taking the credit for Molloy's latest property venture, but David Turner, the Mayor of London, like Carmen and numerous others, was in Molloy's pocket. Then Molloy's phone rang. "Excuse me, gents," he said. "Just got to take this." Sean Molloy listened for a minute or so then said, "What? That slag got Terry and Tommy? Where the fuck were all the others? Oh, my fucking God, this geezer's in trouble!"

Then, without acknowledging any of his potential property investors, he charged through the room and out to the blue Bentley where his handsome young chauffeur was standing waiting.

"Where to, Mr Molloy?"

"Get me fucking home, now!" Molloy screamed at the young driver. "I'll fucking burn the cunt!"

After twenty-five minutes the car pulled off the main drag and into Hamilton Terrace. It was an oasis away from the bustle of the other busy London roads. *My Narnia* Sean used to call it.

"Do you need me to come in, Mr Molloy?" the young chauffeur asked as he pulled up.

"No, go back to the club and see if there's anything you can do for Mayor Turner or that fat poof from the fucking food programme." Molloy was flustered.

As the Bentley pulled away from outside Molloy's palatial home and headed back towards Soho, a scooter pulled out from behind a car four doors down and started following it.

Sean Molloy opened his front door. What the fuck was he going to do with this fucking upstart from the back streets of Kilburn? He took off his jacket and tie then poured himself a brandy, kicking off his Gucci loafers. He walked into his lounge and felt a breeze. He looked across at the patio doors and one of the small glass panes next to the door handle was smashed. The door had been unlocked from the outside. He went out onto the patio and noticed that the cables connecting the CCTV cameras had been cut. Walking back into the lounge he turned on the light and froze. In black letters sprayed over the main wall and straight across his original Bridget Riley striped painting were the words "You're fucking next!"

"Hold off on the kid," Sean Molloy said over the phone to Craig Connor. "I'm gonna need you pair back in London soon as. It's turned into a fucking shit show over here!" Sean needed the Pole and the Scot in London as they were two of his liveliest crew.

"Bit fucking late for that, boss, we've got him here with us. We followed them round the harbour until they went into a side street, whacked the bird and took the boy. He's drugged up and away with the fairies. If we didn't hear anything from Fitzpatrick we were going to throw him into the harbour when it's a bit quiet."

"No, hold that for now. Is the bird dead?" Sean asked.

"I'm not sure, but put it this way, I doubt she'll be making her spinning class in the morning," Connor laughed. "We left her handbag but have got all the proof of identity stuff that she was carrying, including her passport, car keys and phone."

"Okay, well get your arses on a flight back tonight. Meet me in The Nelson tomorrow morning at ten."

"Okay," said Connor. "What shall we do about the boy?"

"Just get rid of him," Sean replied. Sean put the phone down and stared at his newly graffitied wall and ruined artwork. *Where are you, you cunt?*

******

Kim Moore had been half walking, half running, towards her friend's house with Elijah. He was struggling to keep up with her fast, energised, panicked pace, his little arm outstretched holding her hand, and then, from out of nowhere, one of the largest men she had ever seen stepped out in front of her. It was Nowak. She turned around to run and Connor was stood there blocking her path. "Hello, gorgeous," he said as he punched her in the face.

Kim was already unconscious by the time her body hit the concrete, her head bouncing off the kerb. Elijah went to scream and Nowak put a white cloth across his nose and mouth. The boy's little body went limp.

Soho...

It took around ten minutes for the young driver to find a space to park the large blue limousine in Bateman Street, just around the corner from Libretto. The streets of Soho were never originally built to accommodate as many evening cars as they now generated, and the Bentley was one of the larger vehicles using these West End roads.

Joe filled those ten minutes productively.

The chauffeur got out of the car and walked towards the club. He was about to turn into Greek Street when Joe stepped out behind him, pressing a gun firmly into his ribcage. "Act normally or I'll pull the fucking trigger!" Joe snarled into the driver's ear.

"What do you want?" the nervous young chauffeur asked.

"I want a chat with you," said Joe.

Joe had to find and buy a gun in Soho in the time the driver could find a parking spot there, neither of which is a mean feat. The retail offerings in Soho, the vice capital of London's West End, are not exactly overflowing with firearms, and apart from a few bars, restaurants and corner shops the area is mainly comprised of sex shops. So the "persuader" digging into the driver's ribs wasn't a real gun, it was actually a rechargeable, black, silicon vibrator.

"This is the Rolls Royce of sex toys," the pretty shop assistant had advised an embarrassed Joe. "Choose from eight different functions from moderate to powerful. Is that okay?" Joe handed the girl the cash without being able to look up at her. "Would you like some dark chocolate nipples with that? They're on offer," the girl said pointing at the fun-shaped sweets by the till.

"No thanks, I'll, um, just grab some Monster Munch later."

"Turn around and walk back to the car," Joe said, spinning the chauffeur round and walking him back towards his vehicle with the dummy weapon pressing hard into the side of his back. It was all Joe could do not to burst out laughing at this bizarre scenario that he'd created. Here he was trying to find information using something normally used to find a G spot.

"Please, I don't want any trouble," said the frightened young driver.

"Then you're going to tell me everything I need to know or else you'll have all the trouble you need."

There was no point using Joe's weapons of choice, his fists, as he didn't want to beat him up. He needed him unmarked but terrified.

Joe needed the frightening presence of a gun, albeit a black silicone one with eight different settings, to scare the young man sufficiently enough to unload some candid confessions about the goings on within Molloy's Greek street club and details of its clientele.

"Get in the front," said Joe. The chauffeur opened the door and got into the front passenger seat shutting the door. Joe got into the seat behind him pressing the dildo firmly into the driver's lower ribcage. "Now," said Joe, "tell me all about yourself."

Benalmadena…

Kim Moore lay unconscious in the intensive care unit in Xanit Hospital. She was hooked up to a drip and an assortment of bleeping monitors, Elijah's stuffed bunny that had been found lying next to her tucked inside her arm. The left side of her head was swollen and her left eye was badly bruised. A doctor was talking to two nurses at her bedside.

"It is what is known an acute subdural hematoma where a blood vessel tears following a violent blow to the skull causing extreme trauma to the brain. There's a chance she won't come round from this so the next few days are critical."

Another doctor talked with two policemen outside Kim's curtained bed area. "Nobody saw anything, she was just found unconscious on the street," said one of the policemen. "We've got no idea what happened to her. It's strange, she had no means of identification or phone on her, but her handbag and belongings, including money, were untouched. There was a photo in the bag of her with a small boy, maybe her son or a relative, but no one has reported anyone missing. She could be anyone so we need to check for local hen parties and the hotels in the area to see if anyone has been reported missing from one of them."

******

It was just before three o'clock in the morning when Alejandro Lopez walked along Benalmadena marina to his small fishing boat *Aguila* that was moored near the opening of the mouth to the harbour. Times had been rough lately for Lopez and his fellow fishermen. Even though fish prices in general had gone up the fishing limit restrictions, imposed on Lopez and his peers by the EU, meant that they were unable to bring back and sell the bountiful amounts of

71

fish that they used to. Often they would have to throw dead fish back into the sea before returning to shore where their catch would be weighed, because if it was over the imposed weight limit they would face a huge fine making their often dangerous day's work a complete waste of time.

It was still dark as Alejandro boarded his vessel. The weather was looking good so there would be lots of fish and lobsters today, but the sanctions on his trade imposed by the powers that be in Brussels made sure he wouldn't be able to take full advantage of the perfect conditions. It was getting him down more and more every day and getting harder and harder for him to make a decent living out of the only job he had ever known. He drew on his cigarillo, thought about the restrictions imposed on him and muttered to himself, *"Por que quieres matarme tanto? Me cago en tu madre."* "Why do you want to kill me so much? I shit on your mother." He was shaking his head as he untied the mooring line that tethered the boat to the bollard on the pier. He entered the cabin of the boat, lit the hob and made himself a strong black coffee.

Supping the coffee from an enamel mug he looked across at the horizon. The powerful sea looked peaceful and calm. He spoke to the sea as he kissed the silver crucifix that hung around his neck from a black, leather cord. *"No me mataras hoy."* "You will not kill me today." He had a couple of hours until sunrise so he should get going.

Alejandro walked back across the deck, pulled back the heavy, blue tarpaulin that covered his lobster pots, looked down and did a double take. Lying still in among all the tangled nets, empty lobster pots and twisted rope was the body of a small child.

Edgware Road...

"Hello, Frank, what brings you here?" Danny looked across to see his old boxing trainer Frankie Dunne walking into Om Squad.

"Well it ain't the fucking food, Danny boy," Frank laughed back.

"Sit down and I'll make you a cup of tea. What milk do you want, Frank? Soya, almond or oat?" said Danny, grinning at the grimace on Frank's face.

"Fuck's sake, Dan, how do you milk a fucking almond? Ain't you got no cow's milk?"

"You don't get it, Frankie, vegans can't have anything from an animal, and guess what? A cow, last I heard, is an animal."

"Well what about semi-skimmed then?"

"No, Frank. Now, what can I do you for?"

"Have you heard anything from Joe?"

"No, have you?"

"Well," Frank said, looking into Danny's eyes. "Apparently, he's back in the area, causing havoc by all accounts."

"Is he? Why hasn't he been in touch then? I've been worried sick," said Danny.

"Remember you told me he'd never go and see that bird in Spain, your missus' sister?"

"Yeah, I didn't think he would, thought he'd gone off her since she had that kid."

"Well that's where he was and that's where the Molloys went looking for him, so how did the fucking Molloys know he'd go there, Dan? Any idea, son? Because from where I'm sitting something stinks."

"Fuck off, Frank, that's got nothing to do with me. Probably came from Jimmy Moore, you know he's got a mouth when he has a drink, Frank, always going on about how proud he is of his girls."

73

"Okay, so what's going on with you and Sean Molloy, Danny?"

"What?" replied Dan, acting shocked.

"You fucking heard. Now, I'm going to give you one chance to tell me. What's the story with you and Sean Molloy?" Then a voice came from behind Frank.

"Or what, Frank? One chance or what?" Frankie Dunne turned around to see Sean Molloy entering the room with two of his henchmen flanking him. "Come on, Frank, one chance or what? Where's Fitzpatrick, Frank? How about I give you one chance to tell me?" Frank looked at Danny, shook his head then turned to Molloy.

"I don't know where Joe is, and even if I did know where he was, Molloy, I wouldn't have enough crayons to explain it to you." Sean Molloy frowned at Frank.

"See the old man out, guys, this is a modern gaff, it ain't for the likes of him. He's making the place look untidy. Get him out of here."

"I don't need your goons to show me out, Molloy." Frank looked at Danny in disgust and shook his head. "I was going anyway, not really a fan of this place, don't like the people that get in here, they forget where they're from. Fucking almond milk…"

Soho…

"My name's Harry Grover," the young driver said in response to Joe's question.

"So you're his chauffeur are you, Harry?"

"No, not really. Mr Molloy calls me his chauffeur but I haven't passed no tests to be a chauffeur. I'm just a driver really." The rechargeable, black vibrator was digging into

Grover's ribs. It was uncomfortable and made him squirm. *If only he knew what it was,* thought Joe.

"When did you meet Molloy, Harry?"

"At the boys' home. Please, I can't say much, my life won't be worth living. Please let me go, I won't say nothing, I'm gonna be in so much shit if he finds out," Grover snivelled.

"What, more trouble than you're in now with a gun barrel digging into your ribcage?"

"You don't know him. Honestly, I'd rather die here than face him if he found out I told anyone anything. He terrifies me, he's a fucking monster."

"Oh, I know him, Harry, I know him very well. Now, if you do what I say and answer my questions I'll get you away from that twisted fucker forever. If not I'll let Molloy know you've been talking to me and see how he deals with it. So there are your choices. You answer everything I ask and help me to get rid of the cunt forever, or I let Molloy know you came to see me. What's it to be?" Harry looked at Joe with a frightened look.

"Do you think you can get me away from him?" the young driver asked with an air of hope in his words.

"Only with your help, Harry."

Seven years earlier...

Granville House, set back from Finchley Road, was a home for underprivileged children ranging from the ages of ten to eighteen years of age. A large, imposing, red brick building, it was set in half an acre of grounds and had been donated the year after the end of the First World War by Lord Granville as a philanthropic gesture to try to ease the grief he felt at losing his only son in the first phase of the Battle of Amiens, the conflict that, ultimately, led to the end of "The Great War".

Granville House thrived throughout most of the twentieth century, but due to mismanagement causing a lack of referrals from the local authority it was shut down by Camden Council in 1988. The building was boarded up and left empty until squatters moved in a year or so later and it became run down and dilapidated.

In 2005 it was reopened as a children's home by the council and they poured money into it to get it up and running, but again due to budget cuts imposed on the local councils following the recession it had fallen on hard times.

It was at one of the annual St Patrick's Day celebrations at the Irish Centre in Camden that the Mayor of Camden, Councillor Martin Walsh, mentioned Granville House to Sean Molloy.

"The council has spent a fortune on it, Sean. The building alone is worth four times the amount that I could get the council to agree to sell it for to get it off their books. Plus, with the local government grants they'll throw in the care home business is a great earner."

"Sounds good, Martin, but I don't know anything about that game," Sean replied.

"Don't worry about that, Sean, you pay me a decent enough retainer and I can get a team in to run it, all subsidised by the council. Then all you have to do is sit quietly in the background as the 'local businessman that saved the children's home' and watch the money roll in. We can have a bit of fun at the same time. Then when you've run it for a while you shut it down and convert the building into flats. I don't need to tell you. You know the game, Sean."

Sean had known Martin Walsh for a long time. When they were kids they were both skinheads and used to populate the same gangs, pubs and clubs. They remained good friends and, as they got older, though their professions couldn't be any more different, they found synergy in what they did and were great backscratching buddies, the councillor and the gangster roles complementing each other perfectly.

It was Sean that got Martin elected as Mayor of Camden through his various contacts within both local and central government. Sean looked after Martin politically and in return Martin made Sean aware of any opportunities within the borough and beyond, ensuring any planning applications or appeals went in Molloy's favour. Martin Walsh was one of the first members of Sean's West End gentlemen's club, Libretto.

A few weeks after their chat and in a blaze of publicity Granville House was relaunched, with Sean Molloy pictured in the local paper supposedly dressed as Robin Hood surrounded by a dozen underprivileged youngsters done up in a variety of hand-made costumes as his "merry men".

The local fancy dress shop didn't have a Robin Hood outfit. "No call for them nowadays, no one knows who he is anymore," so Sean Molloy was dressed in the closest looking outfit they had in stock to that of the "forgotten" Nottingham outlaw.

"Local Businessman Saves Children's Home From Closing" shouted the headline, accompanied by the picture of the kids surrounding an embarrassed looking Sean Molloy dressed as Buddy the Elf with a bow and arrow.

Among those merry men standing at the back of the publicity photo in the role of "Little John" and waving a broom handle as a wooden staff was a smiling sixteen year old called Harry Grover.

"How was your flight?" Sean Molloy asked as Connor and Nowak walked into his office upstairs in The Lord Nelson just before ten the next morning. Connor started to explain.

"Not too bad, it was a bit bumpy but—"

"Shut the fuck up, Tripadvisor! I'm taking the piss, I don't give a fuck!" Molloy shut him down. "So you went out there to do a job and you didn't get it fucking done!"

Nowak stared at Molloy. He wasn't a fan of the gangster as Connor explained. "He weren't there, boss, not with that bird anyway, unless he was that Micky Clarke that went to Dublin. But apparently he looked nothing like Fitzpatrick."

"Right, I'm gonna break your little bromance up. Grab a couple of the guys each from downstairs and go looking for him everywhere, his old gym, the pubs he used to go in, everywhere. Tell everyone there's ten grand in it for them to bubble him up. Hurt people if you have to but make sure you find the cunt. Don't fuck it up this time!"

******

"I can't believe it, Billy, not if I hadn't seen it with my own eyes."

Frankie Dunne was in his brother Billy's cramped office.

"So, Danny Grealish, whose old man was killed by the Molloys, is in cahoots with Sean Molloy? Don't make sense. The only reason Joe's in this mess is because Dan came running to him about Tommy Molloy wanting dough off him?" said Billy.

"Sean Molloy seems to have outgrown his brothers, Frank, seems he's expanding into other areas, and those pair of clowns are out of their depth and too stupid for where he's going. Do you remember a few months ago when Tony Cheese was selling those knocked off silver picture frames out of Selfridges? He had one left and he was practically giving it away for nothing to Tommy to get rid of it, but he wouldn't take it. 'Why not?' asked Tony. 'Because I don't like the picture in it,' Tommy said. 'You stupid cunt,' Tony goes. 'You take the picture out and put your own picture in. Fuck me, if I go round your house are there loads of pictures of strangers up on the wall?'"

No one in the area knew Tony Queso's real name. He had picked Queso when he fled to London to escape Essex trading standards. He thought it would make him sound Italian and cool, but nobody called him Tony Queso, they preferred Tony Cheese, or sometimes Tony Mascarpone. He was forever looking for a scam and worked a market stall on Whitecross Street. "You like the cigarette case? That's solid silver. My grandfather, God rest his soul, sold it to me on his deathbed." Tony had that inbred Essex trait of being able to be more "cockney" than the real cockneys around him. "Here's me hand, here's me heart, darling."

His latest scam was "CDB Vapes" which were vanilla flavoured vape juices rebranded "CDB" with a picture of a cannabis leaf on the box and hugely marked up. "No, love, it's exactly the same as CBD but a quarter of the price. CBD is a trade name like Sellotape or Hoover so we can't use it, but why have a Hoover when you can have a Dyson? Trust me, these are better, these'll sort all your medical problems out…" The large, tattooed lady studied the small box in her hand then stared back at Tony over her glasses.

"What about the menopause?"

Frank and Billy laughed at the picture frame story, then Frankie said, "Cost Tony though. Tommy had a couple of blokes give him a good hiding the next day for embarrassing him."

"Sean won't even let the brothers in his club up West 'cos they'd show him up in front of all the toffs he gets in there. Terry and Tommy are happy running it round here but Sean wants to be fucking everywhere."

79

Bill nodded in agreement, then Frank said, "Joe asked me why I threw Sean out of the gym, Billy."

"Did you tell him?"

"I had to, Bill, he already half kind of knew. Apparently, I'd let it slip at one of our Christmas do's one year when I'd had a few."

"You never could hold your drink, Frank. What did he say?"

"As I said, he half knew, didn't seem surprised that I'd bounced Molloy for hanging around the younger lads in the showers and making them uncomfortable. Remember, we lost a couple of good little fighters because of him pestering them. Didn't want the gym getting a name 'cos of that prick."

Soho...

"Let me get this straight," Joe said, looking at Harry Grover in the Bentley. "Molloy gets you to drive a minibus from Granville House down to Libretto, full of young boys dressed as waiters who are given free access to booze and drugs on the bus and in the club where they're told to serve drinks, mingle and have fun with the members?"

"Not all the members," said Harry, "only the platinum members."

"Who are the platinum members?"

"The platinum members are the famous or, as Molloy calls them, the influential members. They get their memberships for free and are the only ones permitted in The Great Library. That's where the parties are. It's got its own back entrance."

"Of course it has," smirked Joe childishly. "Are there cameras in there?"

"Yeah, there are three CCTV cameras hidden in the spines of books. I have to check them before the parties to make sure they're working properly."

"What type of cameras are they?" Joe was putting his electrical skills that were born in Kilburn and honed in Mijas into action.

"They've got an SD Card inside them," said Harry. *Perfect,* thought Joe. "But listen, I honestly have to go, I don't want him becoming suspicious. He'll fucking kill me."

Joe took Harry's number and gave him his. "Believe me, I'm gonna bring him and his empire down. I'll be in touch."

The two men got out of the car and went their separate ways.

Harry headed towards Libretto to see if there was anything he could do for the overweight TV chef or the Mayor of London, and Joe went back to where he had parked the scooter. He paused when he got to a litter bin, looked around and chuckled to himself as he threw the Rolls Royce of sex toys into it.

St John's Wood...

Like most mornings Sean Molloy made himself a coffee, then opened his laptop to check the previous evening's goings on in Libretto. He opened the CCTV app and selected the rooms he wanted to view. The Club Bar had been boisterously busy and he watched images of himself taking a phone call and then storming out of the crowded room. Then he watched as TV chef Kenneth Carmen, and David Turner, the Mayor of London, nudge each other as he pushed past them, nodding towards each other and laughing behind his disappearing back. *Pair of cunts!* thought Sean. *I could ruin the fucking pair of you!*

He switched to the room titled "The Study" full of oxblood padded leather chairs, dark wooden cabinets and a decadent marble bar with gilded columns that used to belong to the flamboyant American entertainer Liberace. The previous owner had bought it at auction and shipped it over from Palm Springs.

The Study, as the name suggested, was a quieter room where members went for solitude and to hold small gatherings away from the livelier Club Bar. Although smaller than the Club Bar, The Study was large enough to hide in. There were a couple of members sleeping off the alcohol consumption of the day and taking advantage of the quieter surroundings and large, comfortable furniture, and a few other members dotted around catching up on the day's events on their tablets or the *Evening Standard* newspaper.

Then he opened up the room titled The Great Library. The quality of the camera images were noticeably sharper and showed a large empty room for the duration of the evening. There was no one in there, and why would there be? The next party wasn't until tomorrow night. He surveyed the book lined walls which had been carefully curated. The previous owner had cleverly "cheated" by filling the higher shelves with burgundy, leather bound law journals purchased for £1,800 for every three-metre run. Three large Swarovski crystal chandeliers dominated the air space and a dozen whisky-brown leather Victorian chesterfields sat expectantly empty on the black, oiled oak floor. *The quiet before the storm*, Sean chuckled to himself.

Camberwell Green…

The London borough of Southwark's decision to sell off 132,000 square foot Camberwell Green Magistrates' Court was controversial, to say the least, with fifty-three of the sixty-two respondents being against the sale of the historic building due to the other London courts being so busy. They were running up to three months late with some cases. The money raised from the sale was supposedly going to be "reinvested into the justice system".

It was Martin Walsh, the Mayor of Camden, that first alerted Sean Molloy to the possibility of the sale. Walsh had been at one of the quarterly meetings between the mayors and council leaders of all the thirty-two London boroughs held at London City Hall on the south bank of the River Thames next to Tower Bridge when the controversial sale had been discussed. The decision was made that three property developers would be appointed to submit a tender via sealed bids, ensuring that none of the three companies involved would know how much the other two companies were bidding for the sale. Then it was basically whoever submitted the highest bid won the contract.

The decision of which three companies to appoint was to be made by the Mayor of London, David Turner. The three companies that Turner appointed were "RK West", global leaders in property development, "LPD – London Premier Development", which, as the name suggests, was one of the largest property developers in London, and a smaller company "Limestone Rise", perhaps the most contentious of the three but taken seriously because of the testimonials they had accrued from other London councils, to attest to their policy to deliver sustainable, affordable housing developments.

Martin Walsh and Sean Molloy had done well accruing the testimonials by way of bungs or blackmail from eleven of the other council leaders for Limestone Rise, Sean

Molloy's newly formed property development company. Sean Molloy then targeted RK West and LPD.

A £50,000 bung went to Richie West, the main man at RK West. He was an old associate of Molloy and he also got the assurance that his company would get a big share of the development work on the magistrates' court.

Sean Molloy didn't know Ian Charlton, the main man at London Premier Development PLC, so there was a straightforward threat on the family of the CEO of LPD. These actions ensured that both of the tenders from Limestone Rise's competitors for the magistrate court development were each below £4,500,000.

Limestone Rise submitted a bid of £4,950,000 and when the envelopes were opened by Mayor Turner, to gasps of astonishment, Limestone Rise's bid was the highest. The Camberwell Green Magistrates' Court site was thought to be worth at least £20,000,000.

A 10% deposit had to be paid immediately, then Limestone Rise used the deposit payments from the purchasers of the new apartments and backhanders from eager service suppliers to pay for the rest of the instalments and development.

Sean Molloy had managed to procure a £20,000,0000 development site for the £500,000 deposit money. Among the names of the nine respondents that surprisingly voted in favour of the development of the courthouse were three local MPs, two London judges and Neville Waldron, head of the Metropolitan Police.

Lifestyle adverts for "Liberty Heights", as the development was named, were splashed all over the media promising a superb community of one, two or three-bedroom contemporary apartments arranged around a huge courtyard, with balconies and a lavish roof garden. It even benefitted from its own vegan restaurant and yoga retreat on site.

There was no mention of affordable or sustainable housing. The name of the property company that won the tender, Limestone Rise, had been threateningly introduced one evening in Libretto to Mayor David Turner by Sean Molloy, in its anagrammed form of "It's mine or else".

St John's Wood...

Danny Grealish's life had changed. He had been "taken under my wing" by Sean Molloy and was doing very well for himself. Om Squad was flying and, even taking away Molloy's cut, he was making a lot of dough. Sean Molloy was really impressed with the numbers and saw the potential in "this vegan lark".

"So, someone cuts a bit off a cauliflower, throws it into a frying pan, and just because they call it a 'cauliflower steak' some mug pays as much for that as they do for a proper bit of sirloin? Fucking nonsense, but if they're stupid enough to pay for it then crack on, son."

Sean had also got Danny to take over the food at The Lord Nelson. Dan kept on the existing "chef", Pete "the meat" Knight, otherwise known as "Pygmy Pete" to give him a hand.

"Don't get rid of the prawn and lamb surprise straight away," he said. Danny listened to Pygmy's sage advice. "There'll be a riot, surf and turf is still king round here!" But, just like he did at Rosa's, Danny gradually turned it into a vegetarian and then vegan food offering. It was so popular you had to book a couple of weeks in advance to sample the delights of a plant-based diet in this high end gastropub that used to be among the roughest of Kilburn pubs.

Despite his nickname, Pygmy, at just under six foot, wasn't short. He also wasn't a very good cook, his nickname came because he once made a pot of soup that was so bad that six people got food poisoning from it, and local legend was that a tribe of pygmies were on their way to dip their arrowheads in it! "Oi, Pygmy, give us another slice of that soup," was often jokingly shouted after him when he was walking around the manor.

Weeks later Danny asked Pygmy, "That stew you used to have on the menu, why was it called prawn and lamb surprise?"

"Because there were no prawns or lamb in it. Smoke and mirrors, son, that's what this cooking game's all about." Danny nodded his head and smiled at this culinary advice from a cook who was best known for his food poisoning. "Oui chef".

In addition to The Lord Nelson and Om Squad, the Liberty Heights development potentially offered even further scope, with a restaurant and yoga retreat being built. It was put totally at Danny's disposal by Sean, with the split this time being fifty-fifty.

Kilburn...

"Look, I ain't got a clue where he is, and as I said to your boss if I did I wouldn't tell you anyway. All I can say is that he'd be fucking mad to come back here, this is the first place you blokes would look." Frankie Dunne looked at Craig Connor and the two "lumps" that stood next to him in St Anthony's gym.

"Well I don't believe you, so you're gonna tell me exactly where he fucking is!"

"Fuck off, Connor, you're just a bully like that cunt of an old man of yours was!"

Connor threw a right hand at Frank but, despite his age, Frankie Dunne could still hold his hands up. Frank ducked to his left under the punch and delivered a left uppercut of his own, jerking Connor's head back violently, but the two lumps grabbed hold of Frank while Connor recovered. As Frank tried to get free Connor rained punches and kicks on him, then signalled to the heavies to let go of him and Frankie Dunne dropped, moaning, to the floor.

Connor picked up the jerry can full of petrol that he had walked in with and handed it to one of the other heavies. "Soak this fucking dump in petrol and set light to it, and make sure he's covered in the fucking stuff as well."

******

Billy Dunne was coming out of Ladbrokes on Kilburn High Road, another score wasted on a dodgy tip for a dog. *Fucking thing, stone last, if it weren't for the fact that it had a leg on each corner I wouldn't have even known it was a fucking dog. It was like a different fucking species to the others...* He looked over at his office above the newsagents on the other side of the road. Something was wrong. The lights were on. *I never had the lights on.* Then, as he dived back into a shop doorway, Alex Nowak accompanied by two large blokes came bursting out of his front door looking around from left to right, then they got into a black Mercedes and drove off. *Fucking hell, that was bleeding close,* Billy thought to himself, and then suddenly his thoughts switched to his brother. *Oh my God, Frankie!*

Sean looked over at Harry Grover. "Bring the same dozen kids that came last time, get them there for nine, they should all still have their waiter clothes, and make sure that little red-haired cunt with the stammer don't get lippy with the punters again or I'll cut his stuttering fucking tongue out!"

"That's my little stepbrother. He's only fifteen, Mr Molloy, and that mayor bloke did try to take a liberty with him."

"Hang on, are you questioning me, you fucking melt?" Sean exploded. "I'll put you back where you belong an' all. They're there to be entertained and it's got fuck all to do with you what goes on in there. You just drive the fucking bus!" Sean glared at Harry, shaking with rage.

At twenty-three Harry Grover was a bit too old for most of the platinum members of Libretto now, and his role was mainly to ferry the younger patrons of Granville House down to the Soho club and keep them in order, ensuring that they were dressed smartly and well stocked with ketamine, cocaine and alcohol.

This kid could be dangerous, thought Molloy looking suspiciously at Harry. *He knows too much. This party will be his last, then I'll get rid...*

"Okay, sorry, Mr Molloy."

Harry Grover was terrified of Sean Molloy. He'd seen first-hand some of the beatings he'd inflicted on some of the kids, the acts that he had forced them into, and the power he had in the area. He knew that Molloy was invincible as he had anyone of any importance in his pocket.

Harry watched as Molloy swaggered out of the large front doors at Granville House across the gravel drive towards his Bentley. He stopped on the pavement by the big blue car, looked down at the ground and then turned around to address Harry while pointing at the ground. "There's dog shit here. Get it fucking picked up!"

Kilburn...

As Connor turned to march out of St Anthony's having barked out his orders to burn the club down, a faded, yellow, cast-iron kettlebell smashed into his temple knocking him unconscious. Joe Fitzpatrick had entered St Anthony's by his usual entrance, the toilet window. He knew the front of the gym was probably being watched. He had looked on in horror from the back of the room as Connor gave Frankie a beating while his two fellow thugs held the elderly trainer's arms. Creeping behind the heavy bags, Joe picked up a kettlebell and was close enough to administer the blow as the Scottish bully turned around to leave. One of the other thugs dropped the jerry can and went to grab Joe, but Joe was too quick for him and dropped him with a body shot as he ducked under the gangster's flailing arms. Then Joe jumped on him and started raining punches to his face and head.

"Stop, Fitzpatrick, the game's up, you're coming with me." Joe turned away from the unconscious bruiser that lay beneath him on the ground to see the third heavy standing over him pointing a black 9mm Glock at his face. Joe got up slowly as the man instructed him. "Now turn around and put both hands behind your back." Joe did as he was told as the man clumsily with one hand wrapped his hands together with silver gaffer tape. Then the man walked over to the jerry can, unscrewed the cap and started to pour petrol on the ground. "I'm just going to turn the heat up in here. Bit cold, ain't it? Then me and you are going to see Mr Moll"

He never finished his sentence by the time the circular 10kg weight plate crashed into the back of his head, the weight and force knocking him, the jerry can and gun to the floor. As the huge frame of the man fell down to the ground, Joe saw it replaced by the smaller frame of Frankie Dunne holding the silver plate with both hands.

"You okay, Frank?"

"Yeah, they're big these cunts but they can't throw a decent punch." Frank unwrapped Joe's hands.

"It's getting a bit serious now, Joe."

"I know. I'm gonna sort it, Frank. I'm gutted they put it on you. Sorry, Frankie."

"Don't you dare apologise to me. None of this is on you, these cunts have done all this, you only did what was right. I'll tell you what, if they didn't have a row before they've fucking got one now, son," said Frank as he started to roll a fag.

The main door of the gym flew open and an out of breath Billy Dunne burst through. He stopped and blinking heavily surveyed the scene in front of him, breathing deeply as he tried to take it all in.

Frankie Dunne was sat on a stool pulling on a roll-up with Joe Fitzpatrick sat opposite him on a weights bench. There were three huge bodies scattered across the floor with a jerry can on its side and a black handgun next to it, an orchestra of groans emanating from the contorted men's unconscious physiques. He looked at the two seated men as they stared back at him, then panted, "That fucking dog lost."

******

Tommy Molloy was having a smoke in the garden of The Lord Nelson when he heard the sound of glass smashing from inside the pub. He ran indoors to see a shattered hole in the pub's front door window. Alek Nowak and the two other men that had gone looking for Billy Dunne came running down from the stairs at the back of the

90

closed pub. Alek and Tommy got to the front door at the same time and opened it together.

Had they got there thirty seconds earlier they'd have seen Joe Fitzpatrick headed south on his scooter, straight after launching a brick through the pub's window. Frankie Dunne's white transit van with him and his brother in it had headed in the opposite direction a couple of minutes before after making their "special delivery".

Alek and Tommy couldn't believe the sight in front of them laying at their feet. Bound up with gaffer tape and wearing only their underpants lay three of the firms "top boys", Craig Connor and the other two that had gone off to "sort out that old cunt of a trainer"!

Across the road there were people staring over and laughing at the spectacle. Some of them were even cheering. "'Bout time someone got you lot back. Good on 'em!" one of the crowd shouted over.

"Get them into the fucking pub quick!" Tommy barked at Nowak. The laughing got louder as the crowd grew from the other side of the road. "What are you lot looking at? Fuck off out of it or I'll fucking do you!" Tommy shouted across to the heckling crowd that was mainly middle-aged women with shopping bags.

"Fuck off, Molloy, we've had enough of you lot round here," said one of the women as she picked up a large stone from the gravelled drive of the dentists that was opposite the pub and launched it towards Tommy Molloy. Molloy slipped as he tried to dodge the missile and fell into Nowak and the two others who were trying, unsuccessfully, to carry the deadweight of the heavy, near naked, unconscious bodies across the threshold of The Nelson. This brought more laughter and cheers from over the road, and a hail of stones launched across Kilburn High Road towards the gangsters and their headquarters as the local housewives watched "North London's finest" falling all over the place, trying to pull their enormous, near naked colleagues into the pub while avoiding the volley of hardcore heading their way and being reduced to a bunch of stooges in this real-life comedy show.

Soho...

Sean Molloy was walking through Greek Street when his phone rang. "What do you mean? Three blokes, three fucking blokes? How the fuck can he do three of our fucking blokes? Get rid of them cunts, the lot of 'em." He stopped walking and planted his feet on the pavement. "Tell me this is a fucking joke!" he screamed, oblivious to all the people around him that were staring at this man who was completely out of control. "So, The Nelson ain't opening because all the windows have been smashed? I've only been up West for a couple of hours and you load of cunts allow my business to turn into a fucking shit show!" Tommy Molloy was getting both barrels on the other end of the phone. "I've had enough of you lot up there," Sean shouted, "I've been babysitting you for too long! Fuck the lot of you!"

Sean walked into Libretto. There was an early evening, after work crowd in the Club Bar. The Study was quieter apart from some heavy snoring coming from a leather padded armchair in the corner occupied by Keith Mellor who starred as "Baron Sleepy", a popular character on children's TV. Sean grabbed one of the barmen.

"Wake him up and throw him fucking out. He's not on telly now!" he barked, pointing at the overweight television personality whose whole act was based on him falling asleep in unusual places. Then he went out, walked up the stairs and opened a locked door. This was the other entrance to The Great Library. He was the only person with a key, everyone one else accessed the room from its main entrance on Bateman Street.

Sean helped himself to a canapé from one of the fridges behind the bar area and walked into the main space. It looked very decadent, a throwback to the days when England had an empire. *This bit of the business is good,* he thought. *The other bit's a fucking nonsence with that pair of clowns looking after things.*

Harry Grover walked in carrying an extension ladder. "Evening, Mr Molloy," he called over to the gangster.

"Is it?" Molloy snapped back without even looking over at the young driver.

Harry leaned the ladder against the rows of leatherbound books and extended it to get the height he needed for the cameras. Then he climbed up to check that the cameras were okay and there were no obstructions. Molloy had also asked him to angle one of them at a different part of the room as it wasn't getting as much "action in as the other two".

"Don't be late tonight," Molloy barked. "Nine on the fucking dot." Molloy turned and left through the main entrance.

I fucking hate him, Harry thought as he carried the ladder out later on. But he didn't put it back into the van that had carried it to the club, instead he slid it down the side of the building to be concealed in a long hedge that ran parallel to the brickwork, as agreed with Joe.

Edgware Road...

"Hello, Dan." Danny Grealish turned around to see Joe Fitzpatrick staring back at him. "Mind telling me what the fuck's going on?"

Joe had headed to Om Squad straight from delivering the unconscious gangsters to The Lord Nelson. He knew that

Sean Molloy would be otherwise engaged setting up for his Soho party that evening.

"We'd better talk in the office," Dan nervously said to Joe, leading him into a room at the back of the kitchen. The men sat down on either side of a desk.

"Okay, start fucking talking," said Joe as he glared across at Danny. Danny bowed his head, leaning his forehead on the desk. He knew this day would come.

"He's got me by the bollocks, Joe, by the fucking bollocks," Danny said, lifting his head up.

"Okay, keep talking, and this had better be fucking good."

Danny's eyes welled up as he told Joe the full story about the game of cards, the bungled robbery, the murder of Davy Grealish and the business ventures that he was now involved in with Sean Molloy as a consequence.

Joe was struggling to take it all in. "So you killed Davy?"

"Yes, Joe." At that point Danny broke down sobbing, his arms cushioning his head on the desk. "I killed my old man."

"So what was that bollocks about Tommy Molloy putting the hammer on you for protection?"

"That's true, he did, he didn't know anything about any of this. When I told Sean he saw it as an opportunity. He told me to tell you. He wanted Tommy gone. Tommy's an embarrassment to him and he figured you'd get rid of him for threatening me."

"What?" said Joe in disbelief. "He thought I'd kill Tommy Molloy?"

"Tommy's a bully and he always carries a gun. He thought if you and him had a tear up Tommy Molloy would have to use the gun on you because he wouldn't have a chance otherwise, and Sean would make sure through his connections that Tommy got put away or you'd grab the gun and use it on him. Either way, Tommy would be out of the picture."

"Fucking hell, so you were playing me? This gets worse. Why didn't Sean just get one of his own blokes to get rid of Tommy?"

"He said he couldn't. It was a guilt thing, couldn't directly order a hit on his own brother, family and all that." Joe was shocked by the level of betrayal from his oldest friend.

"Does Rosa know about Davy?"

"No, Joe, of course not. It'd kill her. She's not in great health."

"I noticed that when I saw her at the restaurant. She's lost a load of weight. What do they say it is?"

"They don't know. Doc reckons she's just given up and wants to be with the old man. They reckon it's only a matter of time if she keeps going as she is, so I can't tell her."

The two old friends sat in silence for a while, heads bowed. "What are you gonna do now, Joe?" Danny asked nervously.

"Now?" Joe replied. "Now? Nothing." Joe placed a small voice recorder on the desk. It had been out of sight on his lap recording their conversation. He pressed the "stop" button. "I'm gonna do nothing now, but when poor old Rosa goes I'll be passing your confession on to the old bill." Joe stood up, turned around, and walked out of the room without looking back.

Soho…

The party was in full swing and Sean was delighted to be hosting this decadent gathering of influencers. There were various members of the establishment, Scotland Yard, MI5 and regional police. Also, there were celebrities and politicians, all mixing together with each other and mingling with the dozen young waiters that were walking around the room carrying silver trays. One waiter would

95

carry heavy glass tumblers of Talisker single malt Scotch, while another would have Baccarat crystal champagne flutes filled with Vintage 2008 Dom Perignon on his polished tray. Others would have canapés based on classic English meals, tiny golden scotch eggs with a quail's egg in the centre, mini Yorkshire puddings stuffed with roast beef and horseradish, miniature fish, chips and mushy peas served in a cone as well as tiny beef wellington pies. The caterers had delivered a bonsai version of a medieval banquet and it was very classy.

Then there were the two waiters that wheeled the chrome serving trolleys around containing lines of cocaine displayed on mirrored chopping boards with silver-plated razor blades and snorting tubes.

The whisky-coloured chesterfields were already filling up with a variety of members and waiters "getting to know each other".

Sean glanced up at the positions of the three cameras, rubbed his hands together and smiled. *This is going to be lively, very fucking lively.*

Romford...

"Say when, love," the attractive barmaid said as she tipped the Fevertree tonic into the Belvedere gin.

"After this drink if you like?" Jimmy replied back with a wink.

Romford greyhound track was busy. Jimmy Moore was there with his pals Billy Dunne and Alex Cross on the back of a tip that Billy had been given for a dog running in the fourth race. Jimmy and Alex had known Billy for a long time and they weren't naive enough to think that the night was going to be financially life-changing, or indeed make any difference at all to their bank accounts, except in the negative column. They'd been here before so they weren't exactly planning their holidays around "Expedia" in the 8.45 race, they were only there for the craic.

"You can't help yourself with women can you, Jimmy?" Billy said glancing over at the barmaid and shaking his head at his old friend. "It's already cost you your marriage, you're never gonna fucking learn, are you?"

"I can't help it, Bill, I think I might be one of them sex addicts, like what's his name that played Spiderman, Robert something…"

"Robert Downey Junior?" Alex chirped up. "And it wasn't Spiderman it was Ironman he was in, and you're not a sex addict either, you're just a cunt."

The three friends laughed then made their way to the rails to watch Expedia, who had now gone odds on favourite, perform.

An hour later they sat in the bar discussing their evening. "Well I done alright otherwise," Alex said. "That dog in the last got me right out of jail."

"And you're normally the one putting people in jail, Alex," Billy replied, referring to Alex's occupation in the Metropolitan Police. "But as for that thing, Exterior, or whatever the fucking thing was called, it would have been nice if it had finished in front of just one of the other dogs, not all of them, just one would've been nice."

"Yeah, stone last," Billy replied. "Fucking last! I'm gonna have a word with that Vinny O'Rourke when I see him."

Vinny O'Rourke was a local character that all the lads knew. A painter and decorator by trade, he hung around on the periphery of the dog racing scene, carving out a highly unsuccessful living out of it. He was also well known for his aversion to proper work.

Alex spluttered on his pint. "What? Are you saying that tip was from 'Vinny no work'? Fuck's sake, Bill…"

Then Billy turned to Alex, his voice lowering. "I know you don't say nothing about the stuff you're working on, but–"

"You're right, Billy," Alex said, interrupting his old mate. "And that's the way it'll stay," he finished, ending the conversation.

Soho...

Joe was sat next to Harry Grover in the blue Bentley. They were parked just off Soho Square opposite The Toucan in Carlisle Street when Harry's phone rang. Joe heard Sean's voice on the other end of the line. "Pick me up."

It was two in the morning. Harry's job was to take Sean home from the club, then drive on to Granville House, swap the Bentley for the minibus, return to Libretto, pick up the waiters, lock the club up, then drop the boys back to the care home and return the Bentley to St John's Wood.

"I'll see you at the club in about an hour or so. Call when you're nearby," Joe said as he got out of the car.

Joe walked down Frith Street and into Bar Italia, the iconic Italian coffee bar that opened all night. He ordered a flat white and sat there for a while among the giddy late-night clubbers and merry after pub crowd. He was perched on a high stool against the wall that served as a picture gallery of famous customers and celebrity Italians. An image of Rocky Marciano, the great American-Italian heavyweight stared back at him from the wall, the only heavyweight champ to retire undefeated.

Then Joe thought of what might have been for him in the ring and how the fight with George Wallace would have played out. He had it all in front of him in the boxing game and he knew it. He looked again at Marciano's image and had no doubt he would've beaten Wallace. He thought of

Kim and Elijah, the only good thing to have come out of all this, and how he enjoyed his time in Spain. He'd tried endlessly to call her but the number was dead. *She must have changed her number but doesn't want to give me the new one.* He didn't even know where she was staying in Benalmadena.

He needed to get the job done tonight, then he could go over to find her and see if there was any way he could salvage some kind of relationship with her and Elijah, but in his heart of hearts he knew it was over. She deserved better than him, he had brought shit into her contented world.

How's your luck? I never did anything to anyone, maybe it was karma for me leaving Frankie? Joe pondered as he started, for the first time, to feel sorry for himself. Then he looked to his left over the heads of a couple of revellers at a black and white framed picture of Rocky Balboa punching the air from the top of the Rocky steps in Philadelphia. Joe loved the Rocky films when he was a kid, they were why he started boxing. The picture had a quote from the film *Rocky Balboa*:

"It ain't about how hard you hit, it's about how hard you can get hit and keep moving forward. How much you can take and keep moving forward. That's how winning is done!"

Joe's phone rang and Harry's name appeared on the screen. Joe answered it. "Let's do this," he said as he walked out of Bar Italia with the Rocky theme playing in his head.

Sean Molloy got up very early the next morning. He felt like a child waking up on Christmas morning as he walked downstairs wearing his Versace dressing gown and Ralph Lauren monogrammed slippers. He sauntered into the huge kitchen filled with marble, green tinted glass and chrome. *What a good night* he thought. He smiled to himself rubbing the palms of his hands together as he walked over to make himself a coffee, then he turned on his computer and opened the CCTV app.

He opened The Study first. It was a fairly busy night in there as he scanned the room and noticed a breakfast TV presenter behind one of the huge planters. *What's he up to?* he thought, then the popular star emerged wiping his nose clean. Sean made a mental note to have a word with him.

Then he opened the Club Bar, busy enough but not as busy as the previous evening, he thought, but then a lot of the members from there would have been be in the other space that was on the app.

The Study and the Club Bar were only the starters. He was just killing time before he got to the real reason for looking at the footage of the previous evening, and if the film of the other two rooms were merely appetisers, The Great Library footage was to be a decadent feast.

He grinned, almost licking his lips, as he remembered some of the depraved activity of the previous evening. There were some of the biggest names around in there last night, figures from showbiz, politics, the police and even sporting idols were there enjoying the "entertainment". All of these famous people were now in his pocket. He felt indestructible.

With nervous anticipation he pressed "open" on the first camera. *What the fuck?* It didn't make sense. Frantically he pressed the second camera, same result, then the third camera.

Staring back at him from the laptop was the same image from all three cameras in The Great Library, a black screen with small white text running along the bottom of the screen: "No SD Card Inserted". "No!" he screamed into the air. "Fuck! Fuck! Fuck! Fuck!" He grabbed his phone and rang Harry Grover. The line was dead.

Bermondsey...

No wonder Harry's line was dead. Phones don't ring when they are lying at the bottom of a river. At Joe's suggestion Harry had thrown his phone off London Bridge into the Thames on his way to Joe's, now Harry's temporary accommodation off Bermondsey Street.

While Harry had been dropping the waiters back to Granville House, Joe took the ladder from outside the club and up into the library. When he walked in and looked around the place he was shocked. He took a few photos of spilled cocaine, bloodstains, torn items of clothing and broken glass tabletops. *What the fuck went on in here?* Joe thought.

Then he extended the ladder up against each of the three cameras, unscrewed the front of each camera and removed the SD cards. Putting the cards in his inside pocket he collapsed the ladder, surveyed the room once more, shook his head in disbelief and left.

When Joe got back to the apartment in Bermondsey he opened up his laptop, plugged in his SD card adaptor and played each video of the previous night's debauched activities. He was unable to watch some of the filming as it played out from The Great Library, it was too shocking to watch. It was almost surreal. A lot of these people were household names but it seemed like they were acting in some strange porno film, and there in the middle of it all, like the ringmaster at a circus, was the master of ceremonies looking on from one debauched act to another. The celebrity gangster grinning from ear to ear.

Joe downloaded all the footage onto a memory stick, put the memory stick and cards in an envelope and into his pocket, left a hundred pounds in cash on the kitchen table for Harry, put the key to the flat in the key safe outside, got on his scooter and headed to North London.

Park Royal…

Joe turned off the main corridor and pushed through the doors marked "Ward 5 North". He walked along towards the reception, but just before he got there he saw a dry wipe board outside one of the rooms with the name "Rosetta Grealish".

Joe had gone to Rosa's house to see her, but after knocking a few times her long-time neighbour, the stern faced Mr Parkes, opened his front door.

"She's not there."

"Oh, do you know where she is, Mr Parkes?"

Joe remembered the grim face of the neighbour from when he used to go round there as a kid. Him and Danny were always getting in trouble for kicking balls over Mr Parkes' fence and into his prized rose bushes. Mr Parkes loved his roses more than anything or anyone and spent hours cultivating and looking after them, only for footballs to smash into them from the garden next door, often prematurely "dead-heading" them in the process. Joe glanced down nervously at the bunch of roses that he had brought round for Rosa.

"They took her away in an ambulance yesterday morning," Mr Parkes said, looking down in disgust at the garage bought roses in Joe's hand.

"Do you know where they took her, Mr Parkes?" Joe was overusing the neighbour's name, as even now he felt a bit intimidated by the man that literally used to chase him and Danny down the road.

"Central Middlesex."

"Thank you, Mr Parkes, have a–" The neighbour shut the door cutting Joe off mid-sentence.

Joe knew Central Middlesex Hospital well. Over the years he had been to the A & E department there a few times after fights for stitches or other injuries that needed to be checked out.

As he walked into the tiny room Joe saw Rosa's emaciated figure lying there hooked up to all kinds of machines. He put the flowers to one side and held her tiny hand.

"She's in and out of consciousness," a nurse said as she entered the room.

"What happened?" said Joe.

"She had a stroke yesterday. A neighbour called us. It doesn't look good. It seems she just doesn't seem to want to live anymore." Joe squeezed the little hand and stared at the floor.

"Giuseppe, why are you so sad?" Rosa whispered opening her eyes." Joe looked at her.

"Oh, Mrs G, I've missed you."

"Don't be sad, Giuseppe, I'm going to see my Davy. You though, you need to put on some weight, little Giuseppe, you're wasting away."

Joe smiled as he thought about the irony in Rosa saying that he was wasting away. And with that Rosa fell back into unconsciousness.

Joe looked at the frail old lady next to him as he remembered her as she had been, a larger than life character in every way, a stereotypical "Italian Momma" adored by everyone she met but whose life had prematurely shuddered to a halt the day that she lost the love of her life. She adored Davy and Davy Grealish adored her.

Rosa had always been more of a mum to Joe than even his own mother had been. He remembered the good times when he'd turn up unannounced with Danny for Rosa's Sunday roast. She would always find plenty for Joe. Sundays were the best days when everyone went to morning Mass. The Irishmen and the West Indian men were usually wearing a suit and tie, then they'd go and have a few pints afterwards before going home to the roast dinner, football on the box and a long sleep before a "walk down to the corner" around seven for a few more pints of stout and a game of cards or dominoes.

Joe smiled. "How long d'you think she's got?" he asked the nurse.

"Not long, maybe a day or two if that. I'll leave you alone with her for a few minutes."

Joe choked back the tears as he walked out of the revolving doors of the main hospital entrance. Then his phone rang. He pulled it out and, to his delight, the name "Kim" was lit up on the screen.

"Kim, thank fuck for that," Joe said. "Where have you been? How's Elijah? Is everything…?"

"Shush," said Kim, "I can't talk for long. Meet me at Amy's Wine House in Camden at two o'clock."

"Okay, Kim, great to hear from you. See you in Amy's at two." Kim ended the call. Joe looked down at his watch that showed it was just before midday. *She's safe, thank fuck for that,* Joe thought as he got back on the scooter.

Kilburn…

Frankie and Billy Dunne were holed up in their friend Jimmy Moore's house. "Well, you've really upset them Molloys," Jimmy said, as he made a cup of tea.

104

"Fuck 'em," said Frank. "They sent a firm to sort us out. They were gonna burn the club down with me fucking in it!"

Jimmy gave the men a cup of tea each, then Billy said, "And if it wasn't for that moody dog you told me to back they'd have got me. I was over the road when they came."

"There you go," said Jimmy. "And to think you moaned at me about it, that tip for a dog I gave you. Costly as it may have seemed at the time, it probably saved your life, Bill," Jimmy laughed.

"Fuck off, Jim, that dog's still running," Billy laughed back.

"Tell you what though," said Frank, "that Sean Molloy's some piece of work isn't he? Proper fucked up."

"Yeah," said Jimmy. "And I've heard he's 'behind with the rent'."

"Bowls from the Pavilion End as they say at Lords," laughed Billy.

The three old friends chuckled.

"So what happens next?" said Bill.

"Can't say," said Frank nodding towards Jimmy and winking at Bill. "This one might be a nark."

"Fuck off, Frank," said Jimmy as the two brothers laughed.

"Like that Jewish informer, Mo the grass," said Bill.

The doorbell rang and the three men stopped laughing and looked at each other. "That'll be Joe," said Frank.

Camden…

Joe had been to Amy's once with Kim on a date, so that was probably why she wanted to see him there, he thought. He got off the tube at Chalk Farm and headed towards the bar. As he got closer he saw Kim about fifty yards away walking into the bar. She was wearing a bright yellow dress just above the knee with white and gold McQueen Runway sneakers and large Jackie O sunglasses. She looked great.

He arrived at the bar and stood outside looking around for a minute or so, then he walked inside. Kim was sat on a high stool at the far end of the bar near the exit to the garden.

Amy's was a good place to go if you wanted privacy. It was dimly lit with framed black and white images of the late jazz singer that gave the bar its name displayed on bare brick walls with large, matt silver trunking running across the ceiling.

A green neon sign near the kitchen area exclaimed "Vegan Pie & Mash". Joe looked at it *Fucking vegans!* He thought.

He walked across the room to where Kim was sitting with her back to him with a large glass of white wine in front of her.

"Kim!"

She turned to look at him and said, "Sorry, Joe," then she removed the large-framed sunglasses. He looked at her and did a double take. She looked like she'd been crying, and then he realised that it wasn't Kim, it was her twin sister Karen sat in front of him. He knew then that he'd been tucked up. He was in trouble now. He quickly went to leave and turned into a wooden cosh as it smashed across his brow, knocking him to the floor. Amid piercing screams from the largely female clientele, a second and third blow to the back of the head rendered him unconscious.

Sean Molloy had rebooted the mobile phone that Nowak and Connor had taken off Kim when they attacked her in Spain. Kim and Karen talked and looked pretty much identical, so Molloy had got Karen to call Joe from the phone and then turn up for the meeting.

Amy's was the latest addition to Molloy's ever-growing food and drink portfolio.

London Bridge...

Terry Molloy was finishing up at Borough Market. The Molloys were growing their protection racket into The City and beyond. They ran "protection" for eleven of the stalls there, and every week Terry would go down to pick up, skimming a bit from the top, before handing the takings to Sean at The Lord Nelson.

He walked up the steps by The Barrow Boy and Banker pub and on to London Bridge. As he crossed the road to enter the tube station he saw a familiar face on the other side of the road. *What's he fucking doing down here?* He took his mobile out and rang his older brother. "You round London Bridge?"

"No, why?" Sean Molloy replied.

"I just seen your chauffeur. You know, the blonde fella from the kid's home. Thought he might've dropped you off round here somewhere."

Sean shook his head. "Follow the cunt, Tel, he's turned me over. Find out where he goes and let me know. Keep an eye on him 'til I get a car down there to pick the thieving little toerag up."

Terry kept his distance and watched Harry Grover as he walked down Tooley Street, turned right at the The Shipwrights Arms onto Bermondsey Street, then through the tunnel and right to Snowsfields. He watched as Harry opened the key safe and entered flat number 24. Terry looked directly opposite at The Horseshoe pub. *That's handy enough,* he thought, as he entered the bar, keeping his eyes fixed on number 24.

Joe slowly came round. *Fuck, my head's banging,* he thought as the realisation dawned on him that he was tied up to a chair. He blinked hard as he looked at the ground. *What the fuck happened? What fucking happened? Oh fuck, fuck no...*

It started to come back to him, Karen in the yellow dress pretending to be Kim, Amy's bar, the women screaming as he was brutally hit with fuck knows what, some kind of cosh. Then, from across the room, he heard a familiar voice.

"Getting a bit tasty this, ain't it, Joe." Joe looked up, and sat on the other side of the room, facing him, was Frankie Dunne. He had a cut over one eye and was also bound to a chair.

"Frank? What the fuck?"

"They topped up at Jimmy Moore's gaff. Me and Billy were there. We thought it was you at the door. Kicked seven colours of shit out of Billy and Jimmy and brought me here. Guess it's our turn next, Joe."

The door flew open to reveal Sean Molloy and Alek Nowak.

"Fuck me!" the gangster sneered, "If it ain't the fuckin' Righteous Brothers!" Joe looked over at Alek Nowak. He was sure he knew him from somewhere, but where? "Do you know where you are, you pair of cunts?" Joe and Frank looked round the large room, neither of them saying a word. "No? Well I'll tell you. This is Granville House. Let me tell you something about Granville House. This place was struggling and then I came along and saved it. Yeah, me, Sean Molloy saved the local children's home. Look..." Sean Molloy pointed to a framed print on the wall. It was the front page of the local paper, obviously quite old as the paper was yellowing. The headline exclaimed: **"Local Businessman Saves Children's Home From Closing"**

There was a picture of Sean Molloy in the centre of the page surrounded by the "saved children".

"Why are you dressed as Buddy the Elf?" Joe asked. Sean's face reddened as his eyes narrowed into a snake-like stare focusing on Joe.

"That's Robin Hood you thick cunt. Don't you know fucking anything?"

"I know Robin Hood never nonced his merry men out to the Sheriff of fuckin' Nottingham," Joe replied, staring straight back at the gangster.

"Bring him in!" Molloy shouted at the open door. Joe and Frank looked as two of Molloy's heavies walked into the room with an unconscious Harry Grover suspended between the two of them. They threw him to the floor and on Sean's nodded signal left the room shutting the door behind them. Harry looked as though he had been beaten to within an inch of his life. His face was badly swollen, there were lacerations over both cheeks and eyes, his swollen lips were smeared with blood and, as Joe looked down at the poor boy's battered body, he noticed two fingers on his right hand had been hacked off at the second joint.

"No!" Joe shouted. "No, not him, that kid didn't deserve that, he didn't deserve that..." Tears welled up in Joe's eyes as he looked at the boy pitifully. Molloy smiled.

"He told me fuckin' everything. You've been a silly boy, Fitzpatrick, you've taken something that don't belong to you, something that's mine. Now, where's my fucking property?"

Joe was shocked into a stunned silence. He'd promised Harry he'd look after him, that he'd get him away from this mad beast. Instead he had inflicted hell on him. After a minute or so of silence Joe spoke.

"You're fucking evil, Molloy, what you done to that kid and to all the other kids in here. You're a vile cunt and I ain't telling you nothing. You're fucked, you know that? The recording of what you done with these kids is in a safe place, a place where you'll never get to before it all comes out. Then you and your mates get banged up forever for being the fucking nonces you are!"

Alek Nowak looked over at Molloy. He was never really sure what to make of him. He knew he was a bully and he was uneasy with that, but what Joe was saying was something else altogether, something much worse.

"That's a shame," said Molloy, picking up Harry's lifeless body from the floor by his long, bloodstained hair. Then, reaching inside his jacket pocket, Sean pulled out a small combat knife with a serrated blade and ripped it across Harry's throat cutting him open from ear to ear. Harry made a gurgling sound as Molloy threw his body, face down, onto the floor, dead.

"Right, now it's your turn, old man," Sean said, still holding the bloodied knife and looking over at Frankie.

Park Royal...

"I'm sorry," the nurse said as she looked at Danny. "There was nothing more we could do." Danny nodded his already bowed head in recognition of the nurse's words. "I'll leave you alone with her now."

"Yeah, yeah, thank you," Danny muttered softly, looking down at the frail lifeless figure on the bed in front of him.

The door closed behind the nurse and Danny was alone with Rosa. He pulled the solitary chair in the room over to the bed and sat on it leaning over his mum's body, holding her hands in his. And then he broke down.

There was some kind of closure in Rosetta Grealish passing away, almost a relief. There'd be no more living a lie to her, no need to live a lie ever again. *Now I need to put this right,* he thought as he tightened his grip on the old lady's hands. *I need to do this for you, Mum, and for the old man. I need to do this for you.* For nearly an hour years of pent-up emotion poured out of Danny in that tiny hospital room, and all of a sudden, after years of foggy wilderness, he felt clarity, a lucid purpose in who he really was and what he had to do.

He knew he could never go back to being that Danny Grealish, the chirpy cockney kid that used to help run Rosa's cafe in Kilburn, living on his wits and having banter with the punters as they came in for their breakfast or lunch. That part of him was gone now. Life had put a searing branding iron straight onto his soul, sullying him forever. That life that he had lived seemed a very long way away from him now and he wanted that life back, he wanted his dad back, he wanted Rosa back, but mostly he wanted Joe back. But Danny knew that he could never get any of those cherished things back as that beautiful state of grace was gone from him forever.

The door opened and a nurse came in. She opened one of the drawers next to Rosa's bed and pulled out a plastic carrier bag.

"These are your mum's belongings, Mr Grealish." The nurse paused awkwardly. She was a fairly young and pretty West Indian girl. Then she gushed, "I just wanted to say I'm sorry, she was a beautiful lady. We used to go into her cafe in Kilburn at lunchtimes when I was at school. I didn't have as much money as the rest of my mates and she seemed to know. She would serve my mates then serve me last, taking my loose change which was always well short and giving me my sandwich with a smile and a wink." Danny nodded towards the nurse as he took the plastic bag.

"Thank you, yeah, she was very kind."

The nurse left the room and Danny opened the bag. There were a few bits of make-up and her purse which had no money in it. *No surprise there,* he thought, looking outside at a few of the hospital porters chewing the breeze by a water cooler. There was also a green onyx set of rosary beads. He smiled when he saw them, he had grown up looking at them draped over the framed picture of the Sacred Heart that sat over the fireplace of theirs, and nearly every Irish family's living room when he was young.

Then at the bottom of the bag was a white sealed envelope with "DANNY" written on it in black biro. He opened the envelope and there was the small voice recorder that Joe had placed on the desk in front of Dan in Om Squad. *He didn't go to the old bill with it,* he thought, then he looked further into the envelope. There were three SD cards.

Benalmadena...

"You were very lucky, the damage from the hematoma wasn't too severe and we got to you quickly enough to relieve the pressure on the brain. Otherwise, who knows? If you take thing easy in time you should make a full recovery," Doctor Abrego explained to a drowsy Kim.

"Thank you, Doctor. Is there any news of my son?"

"I'm not permitted to say but the *policia* will be here shortly. They should have an update. They want to ask you a few questions as well. Are you feeling up to that?"

Kim looked back at the doctor. Her head was shaved on the left-hand side and dark stitches bulged from an angry-looking incision.

"Yes, if they have news of Elijah," she said, squeezing the boy's stuffed bunny tightly to her side. The doctor left and she stared up at the ceiling. *Why me? What the fuck did I do? What the fuck did Elijah do?*

Kim had no idea how long she had been there. She tried to remember back to that terrible day in Benalmadena. She remembered hurrying through the busy harbour, scared and almost dragging the youngster along by his outstretched arm. She recalled turning left off the main drag towards her friend Amy Dwyer's apartment.

Kim had known Amy since they were at school together, and they had both emigrated to Malaga a year apart of each other, Kim to be with her mum and, the previous year, Amy to marry and move in with Arturo Lopez and his father.

Arturo was born and raised by his father Alejandro, a local fisherman in Benalmadena. Alejandro made sure that Arturo had the best schooling he could afford to give him.

"If you have an education you will never have to rely on the bureaucrats of Europe telling you from their ivory towers how to live." Arturo was sent to dental college in Torremolinos. "People will always need teeth," Alejandro used to say, hoping it would become his son's mantra before Arturo moved to London to attend UCL Eastman Dental institute on Gray's Inn Road to finish his education. While he was there he lived with a friend in Camden Town and it was on a night out in Camino, a tapas bar in King's Cross, that he met Amy. *Her life sure played out differently to mine,* Kim thought. There was a knock at the door and before she could answer a policeman and a policewoman entered.

"Miss Moore?" Kim nodded back. "We have news about your son and some questions to ask, if okay?"

Kim looked at the two police officers. Their heads were bowed and they seemed unable to make eye contact. *This isn't good, no...* Kim thought to herself. "Tell me, just tell me. What happened to my son?" She burst into tears.

"Okay, he ain't done nothing, let him go and I'll tell you where your tapes are." Joe looked over at Sean Molloy. "If you touch him I swear to God you're fucked. Those tapes will go public!"

Sean Molloy looked at Frank and then back to Joe. *I could just let him go, get the tapes, kill Fitzpatrick then get Frank Dunne and kill him whenever I want.*

After a pause Molloy suddenly turned to Frank. "It's your lucky day, Frank," he said, looking at the trainer. Then he looked over at Alek Nowak. "Get rid of him and leave me alone with this one, but give him a few slaps before you let him go," he said, turning his gaze towards Joe and pointing the knife at him.

Nowak untied Frank and dragged him out of the room through the open doorway. Joe could hear Frank groaning as he was marched along the corridor outside towards the staircase that led down to the entrance of Granville House. Now they were alone.

"So, where are they, Joe?" Molloy grimaced as he asked Joe the question. "The cards from the cameras, where are they?" Joe looked up at the gangster who was twirling the knife around in his hand as he talked. He was out of control.

It went silent for a few moments then Molloy spoke again. "It didn't have to be like this, Fitzpatrick, you could've just come to work for me when I asked you. You're cleverer than all my blokes, you'd have gone far with me, but you chose to go up against me. Well you know what happens to cunts like you that go against me? Do you?" Joe stayed silent. "They get fucked, all of them. Fucked! Now, I'll ask you again. Where are the cards?"

"I haven't got them anymore, someone else has got them."

114

"Oh, really? Who's got them then, Joe, 'cos you're running out of friends. You know we killed the girl and the boy in Spain, don't you?"

Joe fixed his stare on the gangster. He had no words. Then he looked across at Harry Grover's lifeless, bloody body stretched out on the floor across the room and thought of Kim and little Elijah. He looked back at Molloy.

"I'm going to fuckin' burst you for this!" With that Molloy tilted his head back and laughed out loud.

"What? You're going to what? You ain't gonna do nothing, son, you're fucked. Now tell me who's got the cards."

Molloy marched over to Joe and drove the combat knife straight through the back of his hand and into the wooden arm of the chair that Joe's arm was strapped to, twisting it on impact. Joe let out a scream as the blood spurted out, the pain almost causing him to faint. "Who's got the fucking cards? Tell me or I'll cut your hand off, you cunt!"

"I've fucking got them!"

Through a pain filled fog, Joe looked round to see Danny Grealish standing in the doorway holding up a white envelope with one hand while pointing a gun at Sean Molloy with the other. Then Joe passed out.

Benalmadena...

Elijah was still unconscious when they got the instruction to "just get rid of him" from an irate Sean Molloy. "Take him to the end of the pier and throw him into the sea," Craig Connor had ordered Nowak, so Alek drove the silver Audi along to the end of the empty pier then opened the boot and lifted the small bundle out.

At the end of the pier he looked into the black sea water. It was cold and dark with the lapping of the waves against the pier the only sound. There was nobody around when he saw a small fishing boat moored off the pier and looked down at the little boy's innocent face. He thought back to the beatings he took from his stepfather back in Poland. They started when he was about this boy's age. He shook his head, then he clambered aboard the boat. It was Alek Nowak that left Elijah under the blue tarpaulin on Alejandro Lopez's boat *Aguila*.

The old fisherman's first reaction when he found the boy was to get him home then ring the police. It looked as though the boy had lain in the boat all night. His arms and legs were freezing so he needed to get him to his house and into the warm.

Amy Dwyer recognised Elijah as soon as her father in law carried him into the house. She had met the boy a few times when her and Kim would meet for a coffee and catch up, along with other ex-pats in the area.

******

Suddenly the two police officers parted and a blur of activity forced its way through them in the shape of an excited little boy.

"Mummy! Mummy!" Kim gasped as Elijah barged through the officers and threw himself on top of her on the bed.

"Well you never made it to my place, but he certainly did." Kim looked up as Amy Dwyer walked in.

Amy and Kim hugged, then Kim said, "How did he know where you lived?"

"It's a long story but let's just say he came by boat," Amy laughed, looking at the little boy embracing his stuffed bunny.

"What?" Kim looked puzzled.

"Miss Moore," the policewoman interjected, "we'll leave you alone for a couple of hours." The two police officers turned and left the room, shutting the door behind them

"And what the hell happened to you?" Amy asked, gently stroking Kim's bruised head.

Kilburn...

It was dark outside when Joe came round. He was lying on the floor of the room. He wasn't strapped to the chair anymore *Fuck! My hand.* Joe grimaced as he clutched his right hand with his left. It had stopped bleeding but was a mess. It was a woman's voice that had frantically woke him, a foreign sounding woman. He knew who the voice belonged to.

The floor was cold, it was a wooden floor, this was a different place. He looked around and he was in what seemed to be an old disused warehouse. Beside him, just next to where his good hand had been, was a gun. He looked across the timber floor and there, about twenty feet away, was the dead body of Danny Grealish lying on his side with a bullet hole in the middle of his forehead. He was holding the knife with the serrated blade that Sean Molloy had plunged through Joe's hand. He could see that it had been set up to look like a fight. Danny knifed Joe and Joe had shot him in the head in retaliation.

He could hear the sound of sirens that were getting louder and louder as they approached. He looked around him. *I've been set up!*

Joe went over to the body of his oldest, dearest friend. He knelt over Danny and stroked his hair. *All because of a game of fucking cards.* Tears welled up in his eyes and he thought back to when they were kids playing football in

Danny's mum and dad's garden, upsetting Mr Parkes and his rose garden, the day they made their first Holy Communion together when they thought they looked so grown up, and the awful day of Davy Grealish's funeral when Joe had to hold Danny up. "Love you, Danny boy," he said, stroking his old mate's hair. Then he ran across the room to an open doorway and into an empty passageway. At the end of the passageway was a fire exit. He ran to the exit and smashed at the bar that opened the door with his hips and he was out, out into the cold night air, running, running in desperation to get some distance between him and the crime scene.

The sirens got louder and louder; they were close by. He dodged into a shop doorway just as four police cars hurtled past him. Luckily, he had woken up just in time. *Thank you, Rosa, thank you.* The police cars were on their way to the warehouse that he had just run from, the disused warehouse with the cold wooden floor, on top of which lay the dead body of his oldest friend and a 9mm Glock.

Finchley Road…

Karen had told Danny that Molloy had barked at his men to take the unconscious Joe from Amy's to Granville House, but Danny was followed into the orphanage by Alek Nowak who was on his way back from throwing Frankie Dunne out. When Alek saw Danny pointing the gun at Molloy he was in two minds. He didn't like the gangster but he had to think quick. He thought that a gun wielding enemy of his boss would then turn the gun towards him, guilt by association, so out of self-preservation when the opportunity came he crept up behind Danny and hit him over the back of the head with a cosh, knocking him out in the process.

Being unconscious Danny Grealish never felt the bullet that Sean Molloy fired into his forehead before picking up the white envelope with "*DANNY*" written across it.

Then the clear up and set-up began. Nowak was joined by three more of Molloy's heavies. They wrapped Harry Grover's body in plastic sheets then put it into a sleeping bag, zipped it up and loaded it into the back of a transit van, along with Danny's body and a groaning, unconscious Joe. Molloy had got one of his heavies to cosh Joe as he was coming round to make sure he didn't wake up during the set-up.

They drove the van to a disused warehouse that was owned by Camden Council. Martin Walsh had given Sean the keys for it.

After arranging the fight scene between Joe and Danny on the floor of the warehouse, they headed off to Hampstead Cemetery to dispose of the body of young Harry Grover.

At the cemetery they looked for a recent grave, dug up the fresh earth, placed the sleeping bag into the grave and piled the earth back on top. This was Molloy's usual method of body disposal. There was always a fresh grave at Hampstead or Highgate Cemetery. Then Sean Molloy put a phone call in to Neville Waldron, the Commissioner of the Metropolitan Police.

One by one Sean Molloy inserted the three SD cards into the adaptor that was plugged into his laptop and downloaded them. Sean rubbed his hands together as he watched the footage of the night's debauched entertainment in The Great Library of Libretto.

This was really powerful stuff. He looked at the characters playing out the scenes in front of him. There was the Mayor of London, the Commissioner of the Metropolitan Police, at least three MPs from both sides of the house, a prominent High Court Judge and a smattering of well-known actors and sporting icons.

He felt powerful and he felt he had the establishment by the bollocks. With this level of information on these leading influencers of society he could do whatever the fuck he wanted.

Molloy's phone rang. He looked at the name as it flashed up and smiled. "Hello, Neville," he addressed the Commissioner of the Metropolitan Police. "Funny you should call, I've just been thinking about you. Have you got him?" he said as he watched the senior policeman in a very compromising situation on his laptop.

Sean's smile dropped and turned to anger. "What do you mean he fucking got away? I left him on a plate for you, you cunt! What about the gun? It's got his fingerprints all over it, did you get that? That's got him bang to rights!"

Neville Waldron head of the Metropolitan Police was sat at his desk in New Scotland Yard. "We've got the gun, we're having it fingerprinted and sent to forensics to see if it was the murder weapon, but it's looking likely that it is."

"So why is it taking so long?" Molloy barked back. "You'd better fucking find him or it's literally your arse that's fucked!" Sean shouted, looking at the screen on his laptop and slamming down the phone.

Kilburn...

St Anthony's Gym in Kilburn was the pride and joy of Frankie Dunne, and like many a boxing gym in a working-class area the heart and soul of the community. It had been shut since Craig Connor and his two sidekicks had stormed into the place, beating up the old trainer and dousing the floor with petrol in a concerted effort to reduce the former Sunday school to ashes. It didn't need a sign, the heavy chains lashed across the main doors were evidence enough to the locals that the gym was closed to them for the foreseeable future. All except for one local who knew the way to get in through the toilet window at the back.

Joe sat on a weights bench looking around at the gym, dark and silent, the floorboards still faintly smelling of petrol and creaking as he surveyed his old happy place. In his head he went back to how it used to be. He could hear the shouting and groans from sparring, the noise of the skipping ropes whipping away, and the heavy bags being pounded with their chains rattling as they jerked to the motion of the gloved fists driving into them. He looked over at the doorway to the gym and thought back to all those years ago when he and his best mate Danny had finally plucked up the courage to come in, each of them holding the pound coin that allowed you to train. How big it had seemed to them then, full of men and boys training in their cathedral of dreams. To some it seemed the only way out of their otherwise mapped out rundown existence, and yet now, as Joe looked around the dark, empty space, all he could think was how small it looked.

He had tried to call Frankie and Billy but neither, understandably, picked up. He wondered how they were; the last time he saw Frankie he was being led out of the boy's home by the big Polish henchman, and the last he heard of Billy was that he'd been given a beating by Molloy's blokes. *How the fuck did it come to this? Why didn't I just stay here and keep my fucking head down?*

Without even answering the questions going on in his head, he thought back to what Frankie had told him the last time he had been in St Anthony's, the day the bullies had tried to burn it down and failed. *Don't you dare apologise to me. None of this is on you, these cunts have done all this, you only did what was right.*

He thought back to the gruesome scene at the empty warehouse, his best friend lying across the room from him, dead, and the murder weapon lying by Joe's hand. He knew that the gun would have his fingerprints all over it, and he knew Sean Molloy had fitted him up for the killing of Danny Grealish, otherwise he would have had him killed at the scene. So the police would have Joe Fitzpatrick down as the murder suspect. They would be out looking for him soon and naming him in the press, the same police and press that was controlled by the man who had fitted him up for the murder.

Joe felt a throbbing pain as he looked down to his right hand. He needed to get it checked out. If only he could get hold of Frankie's "unofficial doctor" and get him to look at it.

*****

Jack "Jackie" Reid was an ex-NHS doctor who had been struck off for boosting his earnings by peddling Zopiclone, an addictive tranquilising sedative, in the local bars and clubs to fund his susceptibility to pure malt whisky. It was in those nocturnal hangouts that he came onto the radar of the youngest of the Molloy brothers who had cornered the local narcotics market and could do without the competition.

When Jackie refused to be blackmailed into supplying products to Tommy Molloy at "trade rates", Molloy bubbled him up to his employers and the amiable Scottish doctor was dismissed in disgrace. Trade rates to Tommy Molloy meant he wanted the drugs free of charge.

"Jack the Knife", as the boxers used to call the former doctor, was a handy bloke for Frankie to know, often treating his boxers for various injuries without them having to go through the delay of the NHS system, and with an inexhaustible supply of pharmaceutical products from his underpaid former NHS colleagues he would also supply weight loss drugs and fat burning medication without Frank's knowledge to some of the lesser fighters that needed help making weight.

Joe felt in his inside pocket and clasped the memory stick that he had downloaded the footage from Libretto onto. Molloy thought he had the only tapes, the original SD cards, but he was wrong. Joe's phone rang. It was Kim's dad, Jimmy Moore.

Soho...

"What do you mean the gun's fucking clean?" Sean Molloy barked at Neville Waldron at the bar of The Study in Libretto, suddenly lowering his voice and looking around the half empty room.

"There's no fingerprints on it, Sean, it's been cleaned. Fitzpatrick must have wiped it before he fled the scene. Forensics show that it was definitely the murder weapon, but without any dabs we can't pin it on Joe Fitzpatrick. It's strange though, all of the CCTVs in the area were switched off so we can't even put him anywhere near the warehouse at that time."

Sean stared straight ahead. He had arranged to have all the local cameras knocked out so they didn't record his blokes coming and going from the warehouse. The crime scene should have been enough to finger Joe Fitzpatrick as the lone assailant.

"So what are you gonna fucking do about it then?" Sean glared at the Commissioner of the Metropolitan Police.

"What can I do?" Neville Waldron replied uncomfortably.

"Fucking nick Fitzpatrick for the murder. We'll sort the evidence out later. I can't have that cunt running around no more taking the fucking piss out of me, you hear?"

"But…"

"But fucking nothing! I've got you bang to rights on film in a very awkward situation that will get you a ten stretch if it ever gets out, and I wouldn't want to be the head of the old bill parked up with all them criminals in Belmarsh. Could get a bit uncomfortable for you in there once they're made aware of who you are, old bill and a nonce. You wouldn't last a fucking week," Molloy sneered. "Now go and do your fucking job!"

Cala de Mijas…

"But I don't want to go to England, Mummy. It's cold," Elijah Moore said looking up at Kim as she tried to get him dressed to leave for the flight.

"We have to, little fella, to go and see my sister, your Auntie Karen. She's had some bad news and is very sad."

Kim had taken a call from her estranged sister the day before. Karen was in tears on the phone as she explained what had happened to Danny, how Joe had gone missing and was now a suspect for the killing.

"I don't care what they say, I know Joe never did it," Karen said to her twin sister. "Danny was wrapped up with the Molloys and they made me do a bad thing to Joe not long before Danny was killed. I know they did it, Kim."

Karen didn't have to convince Kim of Joe's innocence. Yeah, he could be a pain in the arse sometimes, but he was a good man and loved Danny with all his heart, even though he had been betrayed by his oldest friend. He knew Danny could be stupid and easily led, especially where money and ego was involved, but he told Kim that when he looked at Danny he never saw the man that let him down, all he saw was the little boy that was his best mate growing up.

As Kim drove to the airport with Elijah sleeping in the back she thought about Joe, wondered where he was, what terrible events he had been through and how she had shouted at him to stay away from her and her little boy. She was only doing her job as a mother. Hadn't he put her and Elijah through enough? She thought of her little boy helplessly unconscious and alone aboard a cold fishing boat. She thought about the attack on her as she subconsciously rubbed the raised scar on the left side of her head and shivered.

Kilburn...

"I knew I'd seen him somewhere." Frankie looked across the room at Joe. "Do you remember the fight with that Welsh kid at the Irish Centre two or three years ago?" They were sat with Billy and Jimmy Moore in a friend of Jimmy's flat while Jackie "Jack the Knife" Reid was looking at Joe's butchered hand. Frank, Billy and Jimmy were still aching and bruised from their ordeal but they were okay.

"What was his name? Owen? Something Owen," Joe replied. "Good kid with fast hands."

"That's the one. Had a good long game," the old trainer reminisced.

"What about that fight?"

"See, I got tapped up a couple of days before by, what's his name, you know him," he pointed at Billy, "Andrews, Bobby Andrews? The trainer."

"Benny Andrews?" Billy interjected.

"That's it, Benny Andrews. He's got that gym by the station in Willesden Green. Said he had a good, hungry heavyweight if I could find a match for him. Well, he was a lump, but not really a boxer, more of a fighter. Anyway, he turned up, no boots just trainers, no kit at all, so we kitted him out, boots the lot, and he ended up knocking our kid spark out. Never saw him again until I was strapped onto a chair the other night and he was standing next to Sean Molloy for fuck's sake."

"Was that him?" Joe asked.

"Yeah, as he walked me out he said to me, 'I know you, you good man, you helped me to have fight and gave me boots.'" Joe laughed at Frank's attempt at a Polish accent.

"You sure it wasn't Arnold fucking Schwarzenegger, Frank?"With that Billy and Jimmy, who could be childish whenever they got together, started chirping up.

"I'll be back!" shouted Billy.

"Is there a problem, officer?" Jimmy shouted, in mock Austrian accents.

"Fuck off, you two," Frankie said smiling. "Anyway, he let me go without giving me a hiding and said he would try to help us, then he fucked off."

"Wonder what that's about," said Joe.

126

The funeral...

Two hearses with a coffin in each pulled up outside the Sacred Heart Church. The large crowd was swelled by members of the police force and representatives of the Molloy gang, all looking for the same person in the congregation that may have dared to attend the funeral of his oldest friend and his oldest friend's mother.

The church was packed and overflowing into the car park where the mass was relayed on speakers to those that couldn't get inside. The old man Davy and Rosa had been extremely popular and valued members of the local community, a dying breed, though both had come over from other islands when young. Davy and Rosa were typical of their old school generation, where blacks, whites, Jews, Irish, Italians, Asians and everyone else were welcomed in to share their culture in a North London melting pot, where everyone just seemed to get on and help each other with whatever that day's adversities were. Davy's funeral all those years before was just as well attended as this one for his wife and only child.

The crowd was mixed in colour, age and ethnicity, but they all shared a love for Rosa and Danny Grealish, not the recent Danny who had seemed to outgrow this class of people, but the young Danny, the "state of grace" wide boy Danny that was the life and soul of Rosa's cafe.

They all shared a disdain for the violent family of bullies that had ripped the heart out of their innocent, hard-working community. The representatives of the Molloy gang were openly subject to abuse from the crowd as they were recognised, some of the crowd even spitting at the floor by them. These people knew what the Molloys were and what they were here for. "You'll never find him, he's too clever for you lot," and, "He's coming after you, I hope you burn in Hell when he gets you, you murdering bastards!" were among the barbed lines that were flung in their direction.

Without meaning to Joe Fitzpatrick had become a cult hero to these normal, working-class people, a symbol of hope. Joe had become the David to Sean Molloy's Goliath, the Robin Hood to Molloy's Buddy the Elf.

******

After the moving ceremony the large crowd gathered at the cemetery as the hearses pulled in carrying the two coffins. The graveyard wasn't very far from the church and was already overflowing before the congregation spilled out to make their way across town.

The two coffins were covered in flowers, on Rosa's the largest wreath being formed of the four letters of her name in the green, white and red colours of her beloved Italy. Danny's were simpler with the largest being a heart-shaped wreath made of red roses with a scroll at the bottom simply saying "My Danny" from Karen.

As the coffins were carried through, a single bagpipe player played "Danny Boy". There was hardly a dry eye as Karen, sobbing, held on to Kim at the graveside, alongside Frank, Billy, Jimmy and some other close friends and family. Then both coffins were laid next to each other waiting to be buried side by side, Rosa into the grave that held her "shining light" Davy, and Danny into the grave that they had reserved next door.

The priest said a few words and the coffins were lowered down to much sobbing from the enormous gathering. The funeral had seemed to bring out the spirit in the local people. They saw this as their moment to stand up and be counted, a time to show their community spirit.

Then there was a hush and the gathering turned around and gasped as the lone bagpiper played "She Moved

Through the Fair". The crowd parted in silence as Joe Fitzpatrick, wearing a dark suit with an open-necked white shirt and black Wayfarers to protect against the low winter sun, walked through them carrying two red roses in his bandaged right hand. When he got to the graveside he blessed himself then threw a rose onto the top of each coffin, lowered his head, said a few words quietly and turned to leave. As he turned a single child's voice rang out of the silence.

"Joe!"

He looked over and smiled at little Elijah as stunned representatives from both the police force and the Molloys lurched forward to get over to him, but as they did the crowd submerged them, holding them back by sheer numbers and spirit while Joe walked away slowly through the crowd, his head bowed, and into a waiting taxi.

******

"What do you mean he got away? He walked straight through the lot of you and into a fucking cab!" Sean Molloy was fuming.

"And the old bill, boss," Craig Connor chimed in.

"Shut up, you fuckin' melt! It's a fuckin' embarrassment! Useless the lot of you!" He scanned the four lumps that were stood, heads bowed, in front of him. "Get the fuck out of here and don't come back 'til you've found him. Now get out!" The four henchmen turned sharply, comically bumping into each other as they scrambled to get to the door quickly and away from their irate boss.

Sean looked at them pitifully while shaking his head.

"Connor!" he barked at the largest of them. The huge Scotsman turned to face Molloy.

129

"Yes, boss?"

"You did the work of two men today."

"Oh, thank you, boss."

"The fucking Chuckle Brothers! Now get the fuck out of my sight!" Then, without looking at Connor, he picked the landline phone up off the desk in front of him and rang down to the kitchen. "Get one of your blokes to bring me up a black coffee, and get them to throw a large Irish in it!"

******

Joe stood in a shop doorway just across from The Lord Nelson watching the entrance. He guessed there'd be a big fallout pow wow with Molloy, so he knew that put the gangster in his office and hopefully, any time soon, on his own.

Joe was right. He nodded his head as the four burly men, fresh from a bollocking, spilled out of the pub and onto the street. He noticed that Nowak was not among them. *Good to see Arnie stayed at home.* He smiled to himself as he remembered Billy and Jimmy taking the piss out of Frank Dunne a couple of nights before.

After much talking and gesticulating the four men became two sets of two, the two pairs heading off in opposite directions.

Joe waited. He'd leave it fifteen to twenty minutes in case any of them returned to check anything with their boss. They didn't. After waiting Joe then crossed the road and pushed open the entrance doors of the newly fashionable gastropub that held nothing but bad memories for him.

Joe was greeted sniffily by the maitre d'. Joe recognised him from when they were growing up. John Butcher was a couple of years older than Joe and went to the same school. *Used to hang around with the wankers, including Tommy*

Molloy, thought Joe. John Butcher now called himself Jean Boucher, with thinning black, slicked back hair and the hint of a put-on French accent, he sneered at Joe. "We do not open until six, sir, and you'll need a reservation as we are fully booked this evening." Joe looked back at the man polishing the glasses on the tables.

"Don't worry, I'm not here for the nut cutlets," Joe replied. "Now you carry on cleaning them glasses, son, and when you get good at it they may let you have a go at the windows," then he turned and headed towards the door at the rear of the room that led up to Sean Molloy's office. Recognising Joe, the glass polisher walked into the kitchen, picked up his phone and made a call.

St John's Wood...

"I've got to sell this place, Kim," Karen Moore said to her twin sister. "I can't be round the corner from that monster. I don't know what I'd do if I ever saw him." Danny and Rosa's wake was being held at Danny and Kim's four-bedroom, three-bathroom, contemporary apartment in fashionable Marlborough Place which adjoined Hamilton Terrace, home to Sean Molloy.

Kim glanced over at the picture of Davy and Rosa Grealish smiling back at her from the top of the marble fireplace, then looked back at Karen.

"Don't sell it, just rent it out. It'll be quicker. Come to Spain, Karen, you'll love it. You'll get to see Mum more, or what's left of her. There's a lovely one-bed up for rent in the same block as mine. It's beautiful, overlooking the beach, and I know the owner. You've got to get away from here for a while."

"The thing is…" Karen scanned the room. There must have been thirty or more people there to celebrate Danny and Rosa's lives. Karen stroked her stomach, "… a one-bed's gonna be no good for me, Kim."

Kilburn…

Joe stood at the top of the stairs. It had seemed to take an age to walk up the old creaky stairs trying not to make any noise. The door to Sean Molloy's office was slightly ajar and he could just see the back of the gangster's head sitting at his desk. He'd been waiting for this moment for a long time. Finally, it was the day of reckoning for the gangster. *How's this gonna play out?* he thought as he nervously pushed at the door. As he did so the door made a loud creaking sound as it opened. *Shit!* He ran into the room to pre-empt Molloy's reaction to the noise. He was over at the gangster in two long strides. Molloy didn't move. There was a cup of spilled black coffee all over the table in front of him, but no reaction at all.

Suddenly, he heard a siren, a police siren, pulling up outside the building and lots of shouting downstairs with what seemed like the entrance doors being thrown open.

"Police! Everyone stay still!" he heard them shout underneath him. Joe looked down in horror at Sean Molloy. His throat had been slashed. He was dead.

St John's Wood...

"He was a good kid, Danny, just got a bit starstruck with Molloy," Frankie Dunne said to his brother and Jimmy Moore.

"Yeah, but if you fly with the crows you get shot," Billy replied. "Literally in this case."

"Nice gaff though," Frank said to Jimmy looking around the apartment.

"Yeah, it's okay. No good to him now though, just gutted for my Karen," Jimmy replied.

"Proud of Joe today though," Billy said. "Took some bottle turning up to the cemetery like that."

"Not surprised, are you?" Frank replied. "You know Joe, he was always gonna be there."

"Surprised he hasn't turned up for this. Mind you, he's so hot right now I suppose he'd be mad to come here," said Billy.

"No," Frank replied smiling, looking over at a picture on the wall of a young Danny Grealish and Joe Fitzpatrick suited up and grinning at the camera on the day of their first Holy Communion. "I know Joe, and I think I know where he'd be right about now."

Kilburn...

Fuck! Here we go again! Joe thought as he ran over to the window, the same window he had leapt from months before. He needed to be careful how he landed this time though, he wouldn't be able to outrun the old bill with a twisted ankle. However, like a lot of The Lord Nelson, the old sash window that Joe had launched himself out of on that fateful, life-changing day had been renewed, and when Joe tried to open it this time it wouldn't move. The old wooden sash window was now a UPVC, double-glazed, casement window, and it was locked. Joe desperately tried to open it, and in his desperation he never saw the taser barbs coming at him before they dropped him to the ground.

The kitchen and waiting staff stopped working, looking on in silence as Joe was led down the stairs from Molloy's office and through the restaurant by two overweight policemen, his hands cable tied together behind his back. The silence was only perforated by the sound coming from the back of the room, the sound of a Japanese Damascus knife chopping down onto a thick wooden block. The user of the knife was the only member of staff not looking on at Joe Fitzpatrick's arrest.

Alfie Grover, the new apprentice commis chef with the red hair and stammer, just kept his head down, and with his razor sharp-knife carried on prepping.

Shoreditch...

Terry Molloy changed out of his fluffy white monogrammed dressing gown and back into his sports blazer and chinos, then took his phone out of the locker and saw five missed calls from his younger brother.

Once a week Terry Molloy would visit "Spartan", a gay sauna and massage parlour just off Shoreditch High Street, well away from Kilburn. He always had a massage and sauna, then he'd get changed and go to the bar area to see who he could meet for the evening. On this evening though he would not be going to the bar. It was a voicemail message from Tommy that informed Terry that his older brother had been murdered.

Kilburn...

A small crowd had gathered outside The Lord Nelson when they saw the flashing police car pull up outside. The locals knew that this was the headquarters of the reviled Molloy gang, and when they saw the urgency with which the police arrived forcing their way through the entrance doors they knew something big was going on.

When the crowd saw Joe being led out of the door by the policemen they started to get restless. "Leave him alone, you know who you should be nicking!"

"Arrest the real criminals here!" The people started jostling the police as they tried to get Joe to the waiting car. In the melee that ensued one of the officers slipped on the kerb and fell, to much cheering from the crowd, releasing his grip on Joe. Joe took advantage of this by pulling away from the other officer and then by lifting his arms back and smashing them down onto his backside, simultaneously jolting his hips back to meet the tied wrists snapping the cable tie.

This way of snapping cable tie handcuffs was a well tried and practised technique among the bored juvenile delinquents of the area.

Then, as one officer tried to grab Joe while the other struggled to his feet, Joe sprinted through the crowd and away while the locals did everything they could to hinder the two officers from going after him, blocking their path and nudging the fallen police officer back down to the ground as he tried to get up.

To much laughter and cheers Joe was gone.

"What do you mean he fucking got away?" Terry Molloy was shouting into his mobile phone.

"The old bill, Tel, they sent a couple of fat fucks. They couldn't catch him," Tommy replied.

Even though this was a bad day – he had violently lost his older brother and the business empire that they had grown would now surely crumble – Terry felt a strange sense of relief. He had enough money and there would be no more pressure on him to play the "mad gangster". He could finally be the man he really was and he didn't have to hide his true identity from anyone anymore.

Tommy was a different matter though.

Tommy Molloy was a flat track bully who hid behind people's fear of his oldest brother. He was up to his eyeballs in the very lucrative and dangerous drugs and protection rackets, and without the threat of Sean Molloy behind him he was very exposed and vulnerable to the vultures that would start circling overhead on the news of Sean Molloy's demise.

"You know this is all going to go to shit now, Tommy?"

"Yes, Tel, so what do we do?"

"Grab as much cash as you can get hold of and meet me in The Gaslight in an hour."

Terry knew there was a good chance this wasn't going to end well for Tommy. Even he, Terry Molloy, would now become a target, "a name" that would look good on some wannabe gangster's CV.

"Wanted for double murder!" screamed the headline of the *Brent & Kilburn Times* above a couple of pictures of Joe in his boxing kit. *Kilburn boxer on the run, wanted for the violent deaths of two successful, local businessmen.*

"That's fucking bollocks," said Frankie Dunne throwing the newspaper on the floor.

"They got him bang to rights, Frank. He was in the room with Sean Molloy when they walked in," said Jimmy, craning his neck to read the greyhound results that were now visible on the back page of the paper on the floor.

"So what did he cut his throat with? They never found a weapon."

"Dunno," said Jimmy. "Could've used that karate shit..."

The front door opened and the two men sat up startled. They still hadn't got over the night when their door had been kicked in and they were given a beating by the Molloy gang. Billy Dunne walked in.

"Have you seen that shit in the paper?" Both men nodded. "What are we gonna do now? Can't leave the kid to hang out and dry."

There was a pause. Then Frankie got up, put his coat on and said, "I've got an idea."

"What is it?" said Billy.

"Don't worry," said Frank opening the front door. Then, affecting an Austrian accent looked at the other two and smiled. "I'll be back."

Willesden...

Benny Andrews was sat in his office at Hand to Hand Gym on Station Parade near Willesden Green tube station. He was banging the keys on his calculator trying to make the numbers add up to more than they should so he could sort the month's rent out for the rundown gymnasium. The door opened and Frankie Dunne walked in.

"Hello, Frank, what brings you here?" The two old trainers had known each other from their years on the circuit. There was a network of fighting clubs that were always looking to place fighters on various cards so they all knew each other.

"That lump of a Polish heavyweight I put on one of our shows at the Irish Centre two, maybe three years ago?"

"Nowak, Alek Nowak," Andrews replied. "Good fighter, started coming back in recently. Hadn't been in for a while. Struggled to get fights for him he's so good. What about him, Frank?"

"How do I get hold of him?"

"Well if you park up there..." Andrews said pointing at the chair opposite him, "...I'll get you a coffee and he'll be here in a bit. Got a session booked in with him at two o'clock. What do you want with him, ain't trying to nick him are you?"

The pair laughed. They both knew that if Frank wanted to get Nowak to cross over gyms the last thing he'd do was walk into Benny's gym to do it.

"No, I need to talk to him about helping a friend of mine."

"So who brought the coffee up to Sean Molloy?" The sergeant looked across the desk at Jean Boucher who had suddenly reverted back to John Butcher, dropping the dodgy French accent.

"The new commis chef. His name was Tim, er, Wilson or Walker, something like that. I'll have it written down somewhere."

"Was?"

"Yes, he never came back to work after the day that Fitzpatrick committed the murder. People think being a chef's easy, but it's more than a job, it's a way of life. It's too much for some–"

"Quiet!" the detective shut down the maitre d'. "We've fingerprinted the coffee cup and the majority of the prints on there were from an Alfie Grover. Got a bit of a record for petty theft among other things. He was living in the kid's home in Park Royal that was owned by Sean Molloy, then he went missing. Did this Tim Walker have red hair and a bit of a stammer?"

"Yes, that's him. We used to take the piss out of him when he spoke. He struggled with the letter 'S' so we would have a competition among us to see if we could get him to ask for the sriracha sauce. Was funny." The detective glared at Butcher shaking his head.

"You nasty piece of shit." Butcher was taken aback. "You don't know what that kid's been through, you fucking idiot!"

Sergeant Alex Cross was a drinking buddy of Jimmy Moore and Billy Dunne. He had guessed what Billy was going to ask him about at Romford dog track before he shut him down. He'd been after the Molloys for years without being able to make anything stick. He was an old-fashioned type of policeman, a really good detective, but too honest to do well in today's police force and had continually been deprived of the promotion to lieutenant that he deserved as "Someone like him could spoil it for the rest of us".

So Alex Cross was now resigned to seeing out his days as a sergeant until he could get away from this world of corruption and retire with Sheila, his wife of thirty-two years, to his cottage in Suffolk, never wanting to hear the word "London" again. There was a knock at the door and a constable peered in.

"Sorry, Sarge, there's a big guy…" he looked down at the clipboard he was holding, "…Alek Nowak in reception. Wants to talk to someone. Says it's to do with the Fitzpatrick murders, says it's urgent."

"Nasty piece of work that Fitzpatrick," Butcher opined. "Knew him at school, he–"

"Shut up and wait there!" the sergeant cut across Butcher, then got up and walked to the doorway fixing a hard stare on the red-faced constable by way of a rebuke for giving away too much information in front of a member of the public.

"Sorry, Sarge, thought it was important," the constable whispered to Cross as he shut the door behind him and headed to reception. "He says he knows what happened to Danny Grealish, he was there the night he was murdered."

******

"New Twists in the Murders of Local Businessmen" the *Brent & Kilburn Times* headlined four days later. The paper printed the story of how the late Sean Molloy was now the chief suspect for the murder of Danny Grealish, and Alfie Grover was suspected for the murder of Molloy. They also wrote that Joe Fitzpatrick was no longer a person of interest for either murder. The story was accompanied by a picture of a young, smiling Alfie Grover and another from their archives of Sean Molloy dressed as Buddy the Elf.

Joe Fitzpatrick smiled as he read the headline. He was sat on the apron of the ring at the still closed St Anthony's with a mug of coffee. "He's a good bloke that copper," Frankie Dunne said to Joe. "Good mate of Jimmy and Bill's and as straight as they come."

The next day Joe walked into Kilburn Police Station. He approached the counter where a young policewoman greeted him.

"Can I help you?"

"Yeah, is Sergeant Cross around? I've got something for him."

Borehamwood...

"What do I owe this pleasure to?" Eddie Smyth was at police training school with Alex Cross in Hendon all those years ago and they had remained good friends. Eddie was not as good a detective as Alex but "he played the game", and as a consequence was now the Deputy Commissioner of the Metropolitan Police.

Alex had been to Eddie's lovely home in the leafy suburbs of Borehamwood on many social occasions, always with his wife Sheila who got on really well with Eddie's wife Stephanie. This time though Alex was on his own, and this time the reason wasn't social. Alex gave Eddie the memory stick that Joe Fitzpatrick had given to him two days previously.

"This is going to take a lot of the big boys down, Ed, including your boss, so I'm trusting you to do the right thing with it. There is another copy but I'm hoping this one will get to the right places and I can destroy the other one."

There was no other copy.

"Can I get you a little glass of…"

"No thanks, Ed, I've got the motor and I don't know if you're aware but drinking and driving is still illegal," Alex replied, winking at his old mate. "Me and Sheila will come round soon. I know she'd love to catch up with Steph. We'll have a drink then." Alex Cross turned as he walked through the front door. "This is huge. Do the right thing, Ed."

"I will, Alex, I promise you." Alex Cross opened his car door and looked back at Eddie Smyth. "Oh, Eddie, and if they say they'd like to offer me that overdue promotion to lieutenant on the back of this, tell them I said they can stick it up their arse…"

Three months later…

"Sorry, Joe." Frankie Dunne looked down at the best boxer he had ever trained sitting on the bench with a damp towel on his head. Joe Fitzpatrick had trained like a demon for his comeback, a four-round bout way down on the undercard of George Wallace's bid to win the WBA world title at the O2 in London. Marc Harris had forgiven Joe for going AWOL from the Glasgow fight some months before.

"You never know, Joe, if you've still got it we can go again."

On the night Joe nicked a sentimental points win over a journeyman Spaniard, but a few months earlier Joe would have had him on toast.

There were no more words needed from Frank, Joe knew he was finished as a fighter, it just wasn't there anymore. There had been too many injuries, the ankle twisted from the leap out of the window of The Lord Nelson, the knife through the back of the hand from Molloy while he was strapped to a chair, the months spent on the run, not eating right or training properly, all these things had taken their irreversible toll.

"Don't worry, Frankie," Joe said, leaning back, taking the towel off his head and smiling. "Retired undefeated and I can still wire a plug."

******

Neville Waldron...

Sean Molloy wasn't exactly accurate when he predicted, "You wouldn't last a fucking week," to Waldron regarding his incarceration as a paedophile ex-Commissioner of the Metropolitan Police in prison. Waldron was found dead in his cell in Belmarsh one month after being sentenced to twenty years on very serious corruption and sexual assault charges. Despite being on a twenty-four hour observed suicide watch, he was able, somehow, to hang himself in his cell while the two guards that were supposed to observe him at all times were apparently asleep.

After Waldron was dismissed from his post the Deputy Commissioner, Edward Smyth, was promoted to Commissioner.

Sergeant Alexander Cross was named as "the whistleblower" and given the credit he deserved.

Through Smyth, Alex Cross was offered promotion to lieutenant. Smyth replied on Cross's behalf saying that he had "politely declined" the promotion taking early retirement instead.

David Turner...

Turner was charged with sexual assault as well as numerous accounts of embezzlement, misappropriation of funds, and fraud by abuse of position. He received a sentence of eighteen years and was the first active Mayor of London to be sent to jail. Sentencing Turner, Mr Justice Faulkner described him as "a gluttonous man driven by an insatiable ego, with a salacious lust for all things evil and corrupt."

David Turner died a broken man, of natural causes, four years into his sentence.

Martin Walsh...

The Mayor of Camden and Sean Molloy's oldest friend and accomplice turned queen's evidence in order to reduce his sentence. He revealed all about the property deals and other fraudulent business dealings, naming names both in Camden, where he was culpable, and from City Hall under the jurisdiction of David Turner. In return for giving queen's evidence Walsh received a lenient sentence of six years. Having been assaulted twice, he lives on in Wormwood Scrubs under the constant threat of violence from the other inmates for being a "grass".

Kenneth Carmen...

The celebrity chef was found guilty of charges of indecency and sexual assault was jailed for eighteen months. While serving his prison term at Pentonville, and much to the inmates' amusement, he was put in charge of the kitchen. The rumour was, they said, that Pentonville was going after its first Michelin star. On his release he wrote another cookbook about cooking on a budget, mixed with some prison memoirs entitled *Doing Porridge.* It never got published.

The others from The Great Library video...

Along with the above, several other well-known faces from the world of TV, sport and politics were found guilty of a variety of different crimes involving indecency and sexual assault. They were handed various punishments, from a six-month suspended sentence to huge fines. None of them ever worked in the public domain again.

The only person charged but never to come to justice was Keith Mellor, better known on Children's TV as Baron Sleepy, the posh dignitary with the comical knack of falling asleep anywhere with hilarious consequences. The kids and their parents loved him as he was a throwback to good, wholesome family fun.

At the BBC Keith Mellor, aka Baron Sleepy, was nicknamed "Baron Creepy" for the lecherous way he treated his co-stars who were predominantly male and usually very young, and he was known to be uncomfortable to be around. After being charged with two counts of sexual assault the TV baron became a recluse and the night before his trial took a self-made speedball of cocaine and heroin, both snorted together and washed down with a large bottle of Jack Daniels. Baron Sleepy never woke from that sleep.

Tommy Molloy...

Tommy sent a text to his remaining brother Terry twenty minutes after speaking to him on the phone to arrange their meeting at The Gaslight: *Gunna be a bit late, Tel, got some men that want to buy the drug bit for cash! Meeting them in a bit.* Tommy Molloy was never seen again.

Terry Molloy...

Terry scooped up as much money as he could get his hands on and when he couldn't get hold of Tommy did a runner to Spain. Two years later, in an unrelated incident, Terry Molloy was knifed to death in a club in Malaga. No one was ever arrested for the murder and the Spanish police explanation was, *"tocó el culo equivocado..."* "he touched the wrong arse..."

Craig Connor...

After Sean Molloy's killing Connor went to work for the Sullivans, the North London crime family that had taken over the Molloys' protection and drug rackets. It was the Sullivans that were rumoured to be behind the disappearance of Tommy Molloy. Craig Connor was shot dead when an armed robbery on a Securicor van in Highgate went wrong.

Alfie Grover...

Alfie was eventually found when he was caught shoplifting in Finsbury Park. Homeless and starving, he had been living on the streets and was caught when he robbed a Sainsbury's store for some food. He had shaved his head to disguise his red hair but could do nothing about his stammer.

The judge sentencing him for the murder of Sean Molloy, Mr Justice Chivers, said, "You have been the victim of a terrible life, the depravity of which none of us here could ever possibly imagine. What you did was an act of revenge, revenge for what that barbarian did to you, forced you to do, and, ultimately, revenge for his murdering of your brother, the only family member you have ever had.

Nonetheless, we live in a society that cannot condone murder under any circumstances, no matter how terrible those circumstances are deemed to be."

Alfie was sentenced to a very light six years with the judge taking into consideration his diminished responsibility. While in prison Alfie underwent speech therapy and, though it is not gone completely, Alfie is now able to control his stammer.

Alek Nowak...

Nowak was charged with destroying evidence, for wiping down the 9mm Glock that lay by Joe Fitzpatrick's unconscious body in the warehouse in Kilburn, but treated exceptionally leniently by the judge getting an eight-month suspended sentence for his co-operation and assistance in unravelling the Molloys' dark empire. He got legitimate employment doing security work for Marc Harris on his fight cards up and down the country where he met, and later married, ring card girl Lena Symanski.

When Benny Andrews' struggling gym Hand to Hand eventually shut he moved across to train at St Anthony's with Joe and Frank.

Karen Moore...

Karen sold her beautiful home in St John's Wood and emigrated to Spain to be near her sister and mum. She bought a luxury villa on the outskirts of Marbella where she lives with her son Danny Jr.

Kim Moore...

Kim and Elijah still live in the same apartment on the beach that they and Joe had shared briefly. Kim and Joe never got back together as there had been too much trauma for her to deal with previously. She has resigned herself to bringing up Elijah on her own.

Frank, Billy and Jimmy...

The three great mates still hang around together and are in relatively good health, although a heart scare made Frankie give up the full-time running of St Anthony's, but he regularly pops in there to offer advice, have a coffee and nick the "good biscuits".

Billy and Jimmy bought a greyhound pup from a traveller they met in the bookies. They called the dog "Far Call" after their expected winnings and had a lot of fun racing it around various flapping tracks. The name turned out to be spot on.

Joe Fitzpatrick...

Having resigned himself to boxing retirement, Joe now runs St Anthony's Boxing Club for Frankie. He has introduced Muay Thai and jujitsu to the timetable, almost doubling the membership. There are also plans to add Krav Maga to the curriculum which will be run by Alek Nowak.

Joe received some compensation from Camden Council for Martin Walsh's involvement in the Molloys' pursuit of Joe. The money enabled Joe to buy a modest flat on the same street that Davy and Rosa Grealish had lived on, bang opposite Mr Parkes and his roses. He also "keeps his hand in" as a sparks doing electrical jobs on the side hoping to one day get back to Mijas so he could carry on where he left off with the lucrative CCTV and alarm business and, just maybe, with Kim.

Kilburn...

It was getting late and the two friends were sat down at the end of a hard day in the gym over a mug of coffee. They sat deep in thought for a few minutes, then Joe broke the silence.

"You know, Frank, you and Billy always used to say to me, 'Don't worry, Joe, everything happens for a reason.'" Joe shook his head as Frankie nodded. Joe was thinking about Danny and Harry and Kim. Then he looked up at his old trainer who was rolling a fag.

"But when I think of everything that happened, Frank, I just wish I knew what that fucking reason was."

Printed in Great Britain
by Amazon